SCANDAL ROCKS A QUAINT ENGLISH VILLAGE....

Chief Inspector Morrissey forced himself to Reed's level. He hadn't wanted this close a view of the dead woman's injuries but he felt an odd compulsion to share his friend's repugnant chore.

With hands protected by rubber gloves, the police doctor delicately moved the mutilated head and Morrissey saw another injury, a flattening at the left side above her ear, a discolored splinter that looked like bone.

"Be glad," Reed said. "It looks as if the first injury was a crushing blow, probably with the intact bottle, force fractured the skull in the temporal region. She would have been unconscious when the other injuries were inflicted."

★

A Forthcoming Worldwide Mystery by
KAY MITCHELL

IN STONY PLACES

A Lively Form of Death

A CHIEF
INSPECTOR
MORRISSEY
MYSTERY

KAY MITCHELL

WORLDWIDE®

TORONTO • NEW YORK • LONDON
AMSTERDAM • PARIS • SYDNEY • HAMBURG
STOCKHOLM • ATHENS • TOKYO • MILAN
MADRID • WARSAW • BUDAPEST • AUCKLAND

Acknowledgement
Thanks to the Press Office of
the West Yorkshire Police

A LIVELY FORM OF DEATH

A Worldwide Mystery/October 1992

First published by St. Martin's Press Incorporated.

ISBN 0-373-26106-3

For Satch, Sam and Si

ONE

AT THE SIDE OF St Jude's, along Church Row, the terraced cottages stand neat and tidy, their bedroom windows peering moodily over the church wall. Betty Hartley lived in the first of them, and her hound's nose for gossip would be the death of her.

To view the village from outside St Jude's Church, facing away from the lichened gravestones, with the road to Malminster and the store-cum-post office at the bottom of the hill, Little Henge seems both peaceful and pleasant.

Further up Hill Road on the right, the Walsh house sits pinkly next to the gothic vicarage, while its more conservative neighbours seem to ease haughtily away, keeping their distance. Further up still, and on fine days the squeak and swoop of swings in the small park allow the not quite out of sight graveyard to be forgotten.

From the park, the council estate is out of sight, but its tenants have worn a path through Poacher's Copse on the crest of the hill, and Hill Road itself sweeps widely around the knoll of trees and down through the heart of the estate on its way to join the Malminster road again.

Little Henge hadn't wanted the council estate, and fifteen years of living with it hadn't lessened resentment. Only when news leaked out that Malminster council might use the old quarry as a landfill site, did the two halves of the village come together to send back a communal howl of fury.

There were only two ways to get to the old quarry; through the estate, or past the "posh" houses, and the threat of heavy lorries going either way was enough to demand a truce.

Helen Goddard hadn't even wanted to go to the meeting, let alone be voted onto the protest committee, but putting on a brave face had become a habit. Perhaps the gossip wasn't as bad as she thought; but then from her place on the platform she saw Marion Walsh move to take the chair she had just left, deliberately arranging herself so that her thigh and Robert Goddard's were pressed together. That he didn't even try to move it away added to Helen's angry frustration. Traitor! Bitch!

Marion glanced up at Helen and said something to Robert and they both laughed.

At the back of the hall behind the formica topped tea-bar, Betty Hartley was setting out paper cups with Ida Hodge helping, and as the two tea urns began to steam gently Ida gave her a sly look. 'Didn't think I'd see Mrs G. up there, not with all that talk. Doesn't seem to be bothering her much, does it?'

Betty said, 'Well if that's what you think. Doesn't look all that happy either, does she? And see who's just grabbed her empty seat.' She eyed the back of Marion's head with a mixture of malice and envy. 'Talk about toy dogs.'

'Toy boys, don't you mean?'

'If I say toy dogs, I mean toy dogs,' Betty said tartly. 'Not that he's the only one with his leg up. I could tell you things about that house that'd curl your hair.'

'Go on then.'

Betty laid a finger on the side of her nose. 'One day,' she said, 'one day.'

Ida sniffed, and began to slop milk into cups. She'd heard the promise before.

'If you're that generous,' Betty complained, 'there'll be none left.'

'I don't need it,' said Ida.

'Well I didn't marry the milkman, and if God sees fit to put a bit extra my way, I take it and thanks very much.'

'Thought you'd gone off religion. I can't keep up with you sometimes,' Ida grumbled.

'Never said that, I said I'd gone off *him*.' Both women stopped what they were doing to stare.

Sensing eyes on him the vicar turned. Betty was a burden he could do without, and one day her gossiping tongue would surely cause more trouble than he cared to think about. He turned away and saw Marion lean towards Robert Goddard; and so would she, he thought, so would she. There were serpents in every paradise.

Half of his mind stayed with that thought while the chairman talked on.

TWO

FOR HELEN GODDARD, broken nights were becoming something of a habit as the day's detritus overflowed from her subconscious, and turned into dark dreams. As Robert slept on in the double bed upstairs, she had stood for a minute looking at his face; his bottom lip stuck out as if in petulance, its childishness at odds with the dark stubble that needed to be shaved twice each day. If he opened his eyes, held out his arms the way he used to, would she still go into them?

She moved away. Stop. Stop pretending. Marriages come to an end; why should she have expected hers to be the one that survived?

In the kitchen she stood at the window, with the kettle in her hand, looking across the lawn, past the beech hedge and between the two elms. The slope of ground was such that only the green pantile roof and part of a bedroom window of The Beeches was visible, although from the upstairs window, and with Robert's field glasses, the whole bedroom was open to view; befrilled peach and white, ripe and ready for plucking like the woman who slept there.

Sometimes with Robert.

Yesterday, in his sermon, the vicar had said, 'God is working everywhere, even in Little Henge.' Helen had wanted to stand up, to cry out it wasn't true, that God wasn't at work here, that it was some other force working quietly and corruptingly behind His back.

Not for the first time Helen thought about walking down Vicarage Lane, turning right at the bottom, and then, once she had passed the high brick vicarage wall, right again, crunching up the drive in the house where Marion Walsh spread her legs for how many more men than Robert?

She turned and plugged in the kettle. Upstairs the alarm clock shrilled and after a minute, Robert's feet padded across the landing to the bathroom, the loose board creaking. Mechanically Helen moved about the kitchen until the smell of grilling bacon and toasted bread filled the room. Her hand lingered over the breadknife as she wiped it. Such a sharp blade. Then her husband came into the kitchen and she closed the drawer on it.

Dear God, she thought, I wish we'd never come to this damned village.

He left a little before eight, earlier than his usual time, walking away as he always did now, from any hint of discussion. When he had gone the empty house felt claustrophobic, as if it were accusing her silently of giving in too easily. Uncharacteristically she left the dirty pots piled in the sink and pulled on her outdoor coat. Stamps; she must buy more stamps. It was an excuse, she knew that, but it gave her a reason to leave the house.

When she went into the post office-cum-general store her actions were bordering on the automatic, and she stared up at the still gently shaking old-fashioned bell without conscious thought. Then she heard her name.

'Why, Mrs Goddard, you're early today, it's barely half-past.' Milly, ever-smiling Milly, standing behind the counter.

Helen blinked and moved away from the door, and then it became easy to see why the greeting had been so loud. In a sudden, guilty silence, the two women in the corner by the empty bread shelf turned to look at her with inquisitive eyes. Like the Sioux women inflicting death with a thousand cuts, she thought, they did it with a thousand words.

No need to ask who and what they had been talking about.

The milkman's wife always looked like a slightly tipsy spaniel. Helen could see lipstick stains on her teeth when she spoke.

'Lovely day, isn't it then? I was just saying to Mrs Hartley here, I wonder if we'll have a good summer...'

'The bread hasn't come in yet, me dear,' Milly cut across. Shouldn't be all that long though.'

Helen took out her purse. 'I only want postage stamps.'

There was anger tight inside her head at the knowledge that Marion Walsh's daily and Ida Hodge found her a source of gossip.

Milly's eyes apologised. 'Bread man's always late when you want him to be early,' she said. 'Shop's usually empty at this time.'

Helen took the book of stamps and left, hearing the voices start up again before she had properly closed the door. She began to walk up the hill, her thoughts confused.

Without really noticing where her feet were taking her, she passed the vicarage and found herself outside the Walsh house. She rested her hand on the gate and stared at the blank windows. Behind her the church clock struck nine. Nine tailors she thought, and it seemed like an omen. If it was and someone had to die, she hoped it would be the woman inside.

THE CHURCH CLOCK was chiming again, telling the quarter hour as Ida and Betty followed Helen Goddard's path up the hill. They had reached the corner of Church Row when Betty gave Ida a nudge.

'Look, what do you make of that, then? Looks like she's been in to see Mrs Walsh.' They stood drinking in the new event, their eyes following Helen as she walked quickly on up the hill.

'Well,' said Ida. 'Well, that's not what I'd've expected at all.'

The green wooden bench at the top of the hill was a spot Helen had always favoured, and the comings and goings of much of the village were visible from there. When the children were young she had called it her Trumpton vantage point. Today she seemed to be the only person about, and because there was still a bite to the weather, she turned up the collar of her tweed coat and huddled her hands deep into its pockets. After a while the vicar trotted from vicarage to church, and she had a vague feeling of regret. There had been a time when her attendance had been regular; but that was before she found out about Robert. Now she excluded herself, except for rare visits like yesterday's, and that was something she'd been coerced into after Friday's meeting, by the vicar's long face.

Better to be a Catholic and enjoy solitary confession. Forgive me, Father, for I have sinned... Although it was Robert who needed to confess, not her.

Except that in marriage all things are shared, even sin. The sins of the fathers... Then she saw Betty and Ida emerge from Church Row again and thought: what about the sins of the mothers, how do poison tongues rate on the sin scale? With Ida living at one end of the terraced cottages, and Betty at the other, pity the people in between.

The women parted on the corner, Ida hurrying down the hill on fat, stumpy legs and Betty crossing the road to the Walsh house.

Off you go, Helen thought grimly, in through the gate, take the milk out of its box, and in through the kitchen door, just in time to make coffee. And will you dig the dirt with Madame Marion?

A high veil of cloud began to move in from the west, cobwebbing the sun, and bringing with it a greater chill. As Helen stood and shook creases from her coat, the mobile library backed into place behind the community centre. If she took the short cut home there would be ample time to collect the books she had read and be back in the village before it left.

The narrow dirt path that skirted between Poacher's Copse and the neat patchwork of allotments wasn't a route she often took. In wet weather the path was muddy and treacherous, and even in fine weather she hated the crowding closeness of trees.

'A good place for a murder,' Robert had said when they first came to live in Little Henge, and she had never forgotten that statement even though he had been joking. But today the need for haste had to override dislike.

And in any case there was bound to be someone working on the allotments, and Little Henge was hardly a hot-bed of crime, unless you counted adultery.

BETTY CARRIED the days' milk to the refrigerator. Two bottles were already in there, left over from previous days. With a quick glance to make sure she was not observed, Betty put one of the fresh pints into her shopping bag and closed the zip. Her highness wouldn't miss it, and Betty loved the extra creaminess of Jersey milk even though she always bought homogenised herself.

'That Mrs Goddard came into the post office this morning,' she said as she trundled the Hoover into the sitting room. 'Looked ever so upset, she did. Nice woman, don't you think?' Her face was bland, but the look in her eyes was part conspiracy, part accusation. 'Bought some stamps and walked off up the hill.' She began to unwind the flex. 'Funny thing is, me and Ida Hodge followed her up not long after and it looked as if she'd been here to see you. I said to Ida, that's a turn-up, I said. I mean, you're the last person I should think she'd visit, if you know what I mean.'

'You're an old cow, Betty, do you know that? If you weren't such a marvellous source of gossip I wouldn't keep you on,' Marion said lazily. 'So leave the bloody vac where it is and go and make some decent coffee before I decide just how much more of a liability you are than an asset and fire you.'

From the settee she watched the bony woman go back into the kitchen. She would have to be more cautious where Betty was concerned. Stretching her arms, she swung her legs down and walked to the window, a tall woman, lean hipped and heavy breasted. Although her face was a shade too long, her nose too strong for conventional beauty, she managed her make-up expertly enough to minimise the faults.

Perhaps she should throw Robert back in the pond? It wasn't as though she felt any great passion for him, and at times he could be incredibly boring. He'd probably scurry back to that mousy wife quite thankfully.

Pointless to risk the loss of a golden goose for the sake of a duck. Especially when everything was going so well.

And it *was* going well. Whenever she thought back to her early life, it was with a sense of wonder that she had survived.

She supposed she should be grateful to plump, round Howard with his unusual appetites. He had married her at just the right time when she was on the point of being too old to be interesting, but he hadn't known that. And then he had tried setting up just one arms deal too many with the wrong people, and got himself killed.

Marion was grateful for that too. Very grateful.

Especially for the money.

She wound a stray strand of ash blonde hair into the loose knot on top of her head. Time to reinforce the idea that no one, not even Betty Hartley, was indispensible.

THREE

IN HIS RE-VAMPED OFFICE at Malminster police station, Detective Chief Inspector John Morrissey had a new desk and it felt uncomfortable; not only that but it sent up a smell of newness, a mixture of spirit glue and polish. They had wanted to give him a new chair too, but he had drawn the line at that. The old black leather had worn itself to the shape of his buttocks. When he saw its intended replacement he had sat firm, curling his lip at one side, a ploy that worked wonders with his son, and which after an uneasy minute or two had worked with the supplies men.

Unfortunately for his peace of mind the new chair, a plasticised monster in burnt cinnamon to match the new carpet, hadn't been entirely vanquished. Instead it was lurking in an empty office on the next floor. Such was his distrust of enforced modernisation that when the call came in from Little Henge he was half tempted to secure his old favourite to the desk with handcuffs. Instead, on his way downstairs with Sergeant Barrett at his heels, he let everyone who crossed his path know exactly how ill humoured he would be if anyone—and he meant anyone—tampered with his office.

Little Henge lay exactly four and seven-eighths miles outside Malminster, and green-belt restrictions had proved a successful barrier against it being absorbed into the growing town.

There was a knot of curious faces outside the post office, and a larger group outside the church, as Barrett drove past and swung into Church Row, coming to a stop behind a police Panda.

Inside the terraced cottage Jim Reed squatted at the side of Betty Hartley's body. He had taken off his brown tweed jacket and it hung from the back of a kitchen chair; with his tie tucked inside his shirt and a pair of rubber gloves on, he was checking body temperature, thinning sandy hair falling across the high forehead as he bent forward. Morrissey marvelled for a second that the police surgeon had got there so fast, then he remembered the doctor also had a general practice which took in Little Henge.

Reed glanced up and saw it was Morrissey peering over his shoulder. He said, 'It looks very like one for you, John; cyanide probably, in a fairly heavy dose. Not all that long dead; between one and two hours I should say.' He got to his feet and went to wash his hands at the old-fashioned pot sink, squinting back over his shoulder. 'Pathologist's work now, not mine.'

'Are you saying it can't be suicide?'

The sickly sweet smell of death hung in the air, and with it the sour smell of body fluids. Morrissey wanted to cover his mouth and nose, but knew from experience that in a few minutes his brain would accept the unpleasant miasma and stop sending panic signals. He forced himself to look at the dead woman again; in life she had been plain looking, that much was obvious, but the death rictus had added ugliness. He took his eyes from her and looked at Reed. The police surgeon shrugged.

'It's always a possibility. Not my job to make guesses, is it?'

'Come off it, Jim.'

'I haven't seen a note lying about and most suicides want to make sure someone has a guilt trip. Then there's the cat.'

Morrissey glanced round the kitchen and saw no cat.

Barrett, standing back and with a different angle on the room said, 'Under the table.'

The chief inspector squatted on his haunches and saw the black fur. 'Poor little bugger.'

'If I had to guess, for what it's worth,' said Reed, 'I'd say the cyanide was in the milk. Looks as if she knocked over the bottle and the moggy lapped it up.'

Morrissey touched the wet stain with his fingers. Would an intending suicide put poison in the bottle and not in her cup? He stood up. 'Any idea what happened to the woman who found her?'

'She's in the front room with PC Naylor keeping an eye on her. It seemed the best place. I didn't want her in here, and I didn't think you'd want her to go. With Mrs Hartley dead, she's now the village's chief muck spreader.'

Morrissey raised his eyebrows at Barrett and the sergeant went out of the room. 'I wish I knew how you did that,' Reed said. 'Telepathy, is it?'

'Practice.' Delicately, between his thumb and first finger nails, Morrissey picked up the gold foil bottle-top and held it up to the window. A small pinprick of light showed through. That settles it, he thought as Naylor came out of the front room and into the kitchen. Then the scene of crime team arrived and made a crowd.

Morrissey posted Naylor to stand outside the cottage, and the fresh-faced young constable looked relieved. It was true, Morrissey thought, policemen did get to look younger; Naylor looked like a schoolboy dressed up, beardless and blonde. The chief inspector felt suddenly old; was it really that long since it had been his job to stand outside doors?

He had a quick word with the SOCO team's chief officer, and then took himself to find Barrett and the woman. From Reed's comment he guessed that Betty Hartley had been a gossip. And now she was dead by cyanide. Poison for a poison tongue?

In the front room Ida Hodge was wedged into a sagging easy chair, wallowing in the limelight. If it wasn't for poor Betty she could really let herself go. And with Betty gone, no one knew more about little secrets and private sins than herself.

Barrett had stood his ground in front of a plastic log fire, letting the tide of gossip wash over him, until Morrissey arrived and summed up what was going on behind Ida's avid face without much effort. He cut into the flow tersely.

'Mrs Hodge, why did you come here today?'

She stared at him. What sort of question to ask was that? As if why mattered; it was what she'd found that he ought to ask about, so she answered it with one of her own.

'Why shouldn't I then? It's not as if we weren't always popping in and out of each other's houses.' Aggrieved, the flow of gossip stopped. If it hadn't been for her, poor Betty might have laid there for goodness knew how long. And he had to ask a silly thing like that. 'You'd be better off asking who'd done it,' she complained.

'Done what, Mrs Hodge?'

'Well you aren't going to say it was natural, are you?'

'There is a possibility that Mrs Hartley may have taken something to end her own life,' Morrissey said gravely. 'But at the moment it's only speculation.'

'Never. If it weren't her heart . . .'

'Did she have a heart problem?'

'Not Betty. Strong as a horse. But a heart's the only thing that'd take her that fast. I lays out for the undertaker, and I know.' Becoming confident she could get back into her flow, Ida informed him, 'I know everything that goes on in this village, and I can tell you a thing or two . . .'

But Morrissey was practised. 'Where did Mrs Hartley get her milk from?'

Cut off again Ida glowered. 'From my Ned. Everybody gets milk from my Ned.' She looked at Barrett's notebook suspiciously. 'What's milk got to do with it?'

'Is Ned short for Edward?'

'Edwin. And there's nothing wrong with his milk, it comes fresh from the dairy every morning.'

'Mrs Hartley always bought gold top, did she?'

'Never.' Ida was rattled, and fidgeted. This wasn't the way she had intended things to go, and she didn't know what Morrissey was getting at. Why ask about gold top when Betty always got homogenised? She only got gold cap from . . . Light dawned. Ida almost hugged herself. 'Betty bought red top,' she said.

'The milk on the table was gold top, Mrs Hodge, and as you've said yourself, directly or indirectly it came via your husband. I think you can say how.'

Ida found a trump card. 'It was poison, weren't it? Poisoned milk, that's what you're on about. Well, Betty only ever got gold if Marion Walsh had too much.' It was a moment of triumph for Ida to bask in.

'And who is Marion Walsh?'

'Betty cleaned for her. She's got that pink house next to the vicarage.' She smirked at him. 'Fancy; it ought to be her waiting to be laid out, not Betty.'

Morrissey caught Barrett's look and raised his eyes to heaven, cursing her monkey-sharp brain.

'You can leave now, thank you, Mrs Hodge. *But*,' the word thundered out as she heaved herself out of the chair, 'to pass on knowledge gained during a police inquiry is an offence punishable by imprisonment. If you pass on one word of what has been said this afternoon I shall have no alternative but to charge you.' He watched her face sag and felt profound satisfaction.

'But I...'

'One word,' he repeated. 'I should use the front door if I were you.'

The two men watched her walk past the window. Barrett was grinning. 'You bent the truth a bit there.'

'Let's hope it works.'

In the kitchen the dead woman had been swaddled in a body bag, but work had stopped while a man in cassock and stole prayed over her. Morrissey always felt uncomfortable when faced with outward trappings of faith, without fully understanding why, and now was no different. He watched the clergyman remove his stole, kiss it, fold it, and set it aside. Then the grey-bearded face turned to the chief inspector. 'I've held things up,' he said. 'Sorry. When I heard about Mrs Hartley I thought it was the least as well as the last service I could do for her.'

'She was a regular church attender?'

'No. But that could be my fault as much as hers.' He held out his hand. 'Michael Bartholomew, vicar of St Jude's.'

'Chief Inspector Morrissey.' The clergyman's hand felt smooth, almost soft enough to be a woman's, but the grip was hard.

'Anything I can help you with . . . well it goes without saying. Such a dreadful thing to occur in Little Henge.'

'But not quite so bad in some other backyard?'

'What? Ah, yes I see. No difference of course except in immediacy. Knowing Mrs Hartley makes the thing personal.'

'And can also make some things become obscured.'

Or obscure, Barrett thought, wondering what Morrissey was getting at.

'Indeed. Shall I expect you to call at the vicarage?'

'Sometime this afternoon.'

'Make it around four and share my pot of tea.'

'I'll have Sergeant Barrett with me.'

'That isn't a problem.'

The body was being carried out of the back door. Morrissey glanced under the table and found the cat already gone.

'About four then,' Bartholomew said, picking up the folded silk. Morrissey watched him follow the small procession, head bent. A pillar of good in the face of evil; but the thought in Morrissey's mind was of a blackness of ravens, and he didn't know why.

FOUR

MORRISSEY WAS QUIET. Barrett, keeping pace at his side, was silent too, but for a different reason. He had learned that when a particularly distant look came into the chief inspector's agate eyes, it took a brave man to disrupt his thoughts. They were walking to the Walsh house, leaving the car where it was parked on Church Row. The clumps of sightseers had melted away once they had seen the corpse loaded into the hearse and driven off along the Malminster road, but there were still one or two children, obviously playing hookey from school, hanging about the gate.

Barrett knew they made an incongruous pair; himself neat, almost dapper, and at his side the gaunt, flapping figure of the chief inspector. Only when he was at rest did Morrissey seem to fit his clothes; for the rest of the time he gave the impression of constantly escaping from them, his sleeves too short, and the centre vent of his jacket gaping at every stride. In a lesser man it might have led to mickey-taking, but the stone face was enough to stop any smile before it started.

Morrissey came out of his reverie to remark, 'Horrible colour,' as he pushed open the gate of the pink-washed house.

'It's the green roof tiles that do it.' Barrett allowed a small flight of fancy. 'Mouldy marzipan on a twee birthday cake.'

He thumbed the bell button. The chimes rang clearly but nobody came in answer. He pushed again with the same result.

'We'll try the other door,' said Morrissey moving away, and added grimly, 'Let's hope there was just the one pint.'

The back door chimes played 'Edelweiss', and the house stayed silent. Barrett tried the handle. 'It's locked. But she could be out, don't you think, or am I just sticking my head in the sand?'

Above them a window opened and a woman's towel-draped head declared, 'If you're salesmen I'm not buying anything, so you're wasting your time.' The voice was low pitched and husky. Sexy, Barrett thought privately.

'We're police officers.' Morrissey stepped back to get her in full view. 'Are you Marion Walsh?'

She had full lips, red, even without lipstick.

'What do you want?'

'Are you Marion Walsh?' Morrissey asked again.

'Yes.' She stared down at him.

'Detective Chief Inspector Morrissey of Malminster police,' he raised his warrant card. 'And this is Detective Sergeant Barrett. If you wouldn't mind coming downstairs, we'd like to talk to you.' She stared without moving for so long he felt a momentary qualm. She was either a very cool lady, or there was a fear in her mind. Of what, the police in general? Did she already know about Betty Hartley?

'I'll put something on,' she said abruptly, and closed the window with a bang.

They cooled their heels outside the door until it became obvious that the lady had no intention of hurrying. Indeed, when she finally put in an appearance, it was with one hand on the door knob and the other on the jamb. Her foot, Morrissey saw, was firmly wedged behind the door. Ready to repel boarders he thought, and practised too, by the look of things.

'I hope you haven't dragged me out of the bath for something stupid like a parking ticket,' she said. Barrett studied the strip of body that was visible, and decided that putting something on applied mostly to her face, now made up, because the thin satin robe hid little of the rest of her.

'I believe you employ Mrs Betty Hartley as a daily help,' Morrissey said.

'Oh God!' Marion Walsh threw her hands up. 'What's she been up to now? She can't have slandered the chief constable; she doesn't know him.'

'If we could come inside it would be helpful.'

For a moment it looked as if she was going to refuse, then she stood back and let them pass. Morrissey looked round at the gleaming kitchen with its split level cooker and built-in everything, and thought how much Margaret would like just such a luxury in their own home. When the boat came in. *If* the boat came in.

'You'd better come through,' she said walking ahead of them. In the sitting-room the impression again was of expense; the room could have been designed as a show-piece for one of the upmarket glossies, a carefully mixed designer sundae of apricot, white, and pale dove-grey. 'Sit down,' she said, and it was a command. She curled herself onto a striped chesterfield, her arms outspread along the back.

The thing that impressed itself most on Morrissey's consciousness was the room's anonymity. He looked around and found none of the trivia of living; no photographs, no untidy pile of newspapers and magazines. Even the books in the bookcase looked untouched.

A woman who didn't want to be known, he decided as he loosed his straining jacket button and sat down facing her. Barrett hesitated before he lowered himself onto a straight-backed chair, both looking and feeling ill at ease.

'So what has Betty done?' Marion Walsh said lazily. 'Because whatever it is, I don't see how I can help you. I wouldn't call myself her confidante, I promise you. We have a strictly employer/employee relationship, and I have a feeling even that won't be for very much longer.'

'Her work dissatisfies you?'

'*She* dissatisfies me. And since you're here, I should imagine you're going to add fuel to the fire.'

'What fire would that be?'

'Not being bothered about time-keeping, coming late, leaving early. Gossiping about all and sundry. And not only to me. Every juicy little tit-bit is round the village like a forest fire.' She opened the lid of a white onyx cigarette box and offered it, saying: 'Aren't you good?' when they both refused, and lighting one herself. She inhaled deeply. The smoke drifted across the space between them. Morrissey wafted his hand at it.

When she leaned forward, her heavy breasts fell against the thin silk. 'Come on then, don't keep me in suspense, tell me what she's been up to.'

'She's dead,' Morrissey said bluntly, disliking the blatant exhibitionism, and wanting to shock in return.

Her eyes widened and flickered, but that was all the reaction she showed as she leaned back and took a deeper drag on the cigarette, her eyes going from one to the other.

'That was rather naughty of you wasn't it?' she said finally. 'Unkind. Poor Betty. However, I shan't retract a word of what I said. What happened to her?'

'I can only say we are treating her death as suspicious. Did you often give Mrs Hartley milk that you hadn't used yourself?'

'No. But I recognise that Betty often relieved me of
the odd bottle she thought I wouldn't miss. Is that the
same thing?'

'You never reprimanded her?'

'It didn't seem worth the effort. She didn't take
anything else, or at least, only other odd bits from the
kitchen. Party leftovers, that sort of thing.'

'How long had she worked for you?'

'A year or so.'

'And you've lived here yourself for how long?'

'A year or so.' She stubbed out the cigarette. 'She
was here this morning and left at twelve-thirty, and
she was perfectly healthy then, I promise you. I
haven't seen her since, I'm sorry I can't be more help.'
She stood, signalling an end to the interview. Morrissey stayed where he was.

'How did Mr Walsh feel about Mrs Hartley?'

'Mr Walsh?' She laughed. 'I'm afraid only a me-
dium could tell you that.'

'He's dead?'

'I sincerely hope so, because he's certainly buried.
Now if you don't mind . . . ?'

'Where?'

'God but you're a nosey lot! In some corner of a
foreign field that will be forever England. Is that the
way it goes?'

'Something like that. Which foreign field?'

'Idi Amin took exception to one of his Ugandan
business trips. Fortunately he was well insured. Now
if you don't mind I have other things to do.'

Poor devil, Morrissey thought as he stood up. Heads or tails would still have made Walsh a loser. Out loud he said, 'I need to have a look at the rest of your milk. In fact I shall have to take it away with me, and I'd like you to show me where the milkman leaves it each morning. If you don't mind.'

'What on earth do you want it for?'

'To test it for toxic substances.'

Her face lost some of its composure, then froze again. 'Poison? Is that what you mean by toxic substances?'

'We have good reason to think Mrs Hartley may have taken poison either deliberately or otherwise.'

'And you're suggesting it was in the milk she took from here? Ridiculous.' She flung out of the room with Barrett following. Morrissey came more leisurely. She took a full pint, and a half bottle of milk from the refrigerator.

'I take two pints a day, but there should have been another pint left from yesterday,' she said icily. 'I suppose that's the one we've been talking about.' She thrust the two bottles at Barrett. 'I think you'll find it perfectly innocent. As you see, I've already used quite a lot.'

'I hope so,' Morrissey said somberly. 'Because otherwise we have to face the possibility that the poison was intended for you.'

This time her face showed nothing. 'I think that would be an error on your part, Inspector, but thank you for your concern.' She crossed the kitchen, the light from the glass door passing through the flimsy robe, showing the shape of her body. A woman to lust after Morrissey thought, rather than to love.

She held open the door. 'You'll see there's a box on the wall to hold the milk,' she said. 'It foils the cats, there are a lot of them about.'

Was she implying two-legged as well as four Morrissey wondered as he stepped outside. 'I shall need to see you again, so if you decide to stay with friends for a few days, let me know where you've gone.'

'You'll find me here, I'm really not the nervous type.'

You can say that again he thought as he walked away.

'A very cool lady,' Barrett said as they went through the gate. 'I wonder what sort of a sex life she has. A bit one sided I should think.'

'God!' Morrissey complained. 'That's all your age group ever think about. I'm surprised you have the strength left to work.'

'It's not thinking about it that takes it out of you,' Barrett corrected, and added thoughtfully, 'But I wouldn't like to be married to that lady. Did you know black widow spiders eat their mates when they've finished bonking?'

'Unlucky buggers aren't they?' Morrissey said. 'I wonder what they do with the bones.'

FIVE

IT AMUSED Marion Walsh to upturn the milk bottle and watch its creamy contents swirl down the sink. She couldn't weep crocodile tears for Betty; if the damned woman had kept her pilfering fingers to herself she would still be alive. It didn't, at that point, strike her that she herself might then be dead; instead her mind had given prime importance to convincing the police that the milk had been tampered with after it had been filched, and not before. Thank God that boob struck sergeant had kept his eyes on her cleavage. He had gone off quite happily with yesterday's milk, and not a thought in his head that the body he was ogling so thoroughly might be blocking his view of one more bottle.

That was one sure thing about dear departed Betty, she was always predictable; when she took the odd bottle home it was always the freshest, anything else would have gone against her nature.

And with the second pint from that morning's delivery washed away, Marion knew that no one could prove it concerned her at all. She rinsed the bottle, and rinsed it again; only then did she hold the cap up against the light and see the pinprick.

Her reaction was annoyance rather than fear. To have the police crowding her doorstep, peering into her life, would disturb—destroy?—everything she had worked for so carefully.

And if the poison had been meant for her, then Marion was quite certain of its source. Her surprise lay not in knowing Helen Goddard might want to go to such lengths, but that she would have the courage.

It had been Betty's last unknowing service to notice Robert's wife coming away from the house that morning. It was ironic in an off-beat way that, in its last piece of gossip, the daily's barbed tongue had come to good use. Marion's fingers crushed the gold foil and dropped it into the waste bin.

Finding someone else to do the cleaning was going to be a damn nuisance. And so was taking the risk of going to see that dratted little mouse-woman, but there was no way round it.

Her approach was direct and without caution; a furious striding up Vicarage Lane to the Goddard house, and her finger deliberately kept on the bell-push even when the door began to open. Helen Goddard regarded her first with disbelief and then with anger.

Knowing Helen would close the door in her face, Marion set her weight against it. 'Believe me,' she snapped, 'you're the last person I'd want to visit in normal circumstances, but I know about the milk.'

Helen said through the crack, 'What milk?'

'The milk you added poison to.' Marion shoved hard and was in the hall, saying with heavy sarcasm, 'Don't bother to offer me coffee, I seem to have lost my taste for it.'

Helen was red. 'I wouldn't offer you anything. Get out.' The push she gave Marion earned a stinging slap in return, and she was half-pushed, half-dragged into the living-room.

'Sit.' A final push sent Helen onto the settee. 'Did you really think you'd get away with poisoning my milk? I suppose when you saw the village swarming with policemen you thought it had worked. The amusing thing is, you needn't have bothered—I'd already decided to send your husband home. If there was an award for the most boring adulterer he'd win it. I can't think why you want him back so badly. Still, I suppose a mousy frump like you can't expect to attract very much.'

The sense of anger and humiliation was a physical pain and Helen wanted to strike back. 'Trollop!' she spat, struggling to her feet. 'Whore! I wish I could kill you! I'd do it gladly.'

'I know,' Marion said. 'But then you've already tried. Unfortunately my cleaner died instead. You killed Betty Hartley: how do you feel about that? Not a great loss to the community perhaps, but not what you intended either.' She put her hand in the centre of Helen's chest and thrust hard, sending her sprawling onto the settee again. 'Sit down, you look quite ill.'

There was now confusion mixed with the anger in
Helen's mind. She remembered having wished Marion Walsh dead that morning as the church clock
chimed; and wishing it earlier when she'd had the
breadknife in her hand. The memory returned of
herself standing outside Marion's back door, her
hand on a milk bottle. She seemed to have waited a
long time but no one had answered the doorbell.

She dug her fingers into the fabric of the settee. Her
voice was thin. 'Isn't it enough that you whore for my
husband, do you want me to give up my home too, is
that why you're here?'

'My advice,' said Marion ignoring her, 'is to get rid
of any poison there is left, and make damn sure the
bottle can't be found, because Betty wasn't the only
one to see you this morning, and eventually the police will turn up on your doorstep. Do you understand what I'm telling you?'

No, Helen thought, head spinning, no she damn
well didn't understand. Bottles, poison! One of them
was mad. Mad Marion and Robert Hood she
thought, and began to laugh on a high-pitched note.

Marion watched and wondered if the woman before her was fully sane, because if not, the affair with
Robert could prove to be the biggest mistake she had
ever made.

It was a shock, when she returned to The Beeches,
to find plain-clothesmen dusting for fingerprints on
the gate and the milk holder by the back door. For the
first time, recognition that she had narrowly missed

death struck her forcibly, and letting herself into the house she felt chilled.

Morrissey, sitting in the high-ceilinged study of the vicarage, was chilled too, but it was a different chill, a dank, seeping cold that seemed to be part of the building. Barrett, legs crossed, foot swinging gently, seemed not to notice. Margaret insisted houses had their own atmosphere, that she could tell what the people who lived in them were like just by soaking it up. What would she make of this? Morrissey put his empty teacup on the low table and rubbed his hands together.

'You're cold, Chief Inspector.' Bartholomew saw the action and turned up the gas fire. 'Old houses are something one becomes inured to, and it's easy to forget other people are more accustomed to central heating.'

Morrissey's grunt could have been agreement or not as his legs stretched out towards the heat. He came back to the subject of Betty Hartley. 'I don't know much about these things, but if Mrs Hartley wasn't one of your regular churchgoers, why did you find it important, or even necessary, to read the last rites?'

'You're not a communicant yourself?'

Nice try, thought Morrissey, who intended keeping his faith, or lack of it, to himself. 'Mrs Hartley was?'

'No. She was most in evidence at other occasions; weddings, christenings, burial services. Keeping up with village life, I believe she called it.'

'And what did you call it?'

'I'm what is euphemistically called a liberal thinker where church matters are concerned. I believe the reason is less important than the presence.'

'And all sins are forgiven?'

'One man's sin is another man's custom.' Bartholomew too could be evasive.

'The important question is which of your parishioners might have wished Mrs Hartley dead?' said Morrissey. 'Wished it enough to do something about it.'

'I can't believe it of any of them,' Bartholomew was firm. 'Mrs Hartley was a nuisance to many people, but I don't believe she was a threat. Gossips are tolerated in small villages, always have been. It's the way news gets around.'

'A truth that's told with bad intent beats all the lies you can invent,' quoted Morrissey.

The vicar nodded. 'Blake. An unorthodox thinker with a great deal of insight, but although I take your point, even gossip can have a good side. It can for example be a very effective deterrent against adultery in a community of this size. No one wants to be found out.'

'I didn't think anyone bothered about it these days,' Barrett said. 'It seems pretty harmless compared to mugging old ladies.'

'Or poisoning them,' said Morrissey. 'I suppose Mrs Hartley would have known who was sleeping with who?'

'As the sergeant implied, it's hardly grounds for murder.'

'The woman Mrs Hartley worked for, Marion Walsh, is she a church attender?'

Bartholomew shook his head. 'No. That I can tell you without fear of breaching a confidence.'

Morrissey said, 'An attractive woman on her own, she must worry a few wives.'

'Possibly.'

'No one wife in particular, though.'

'I'm sorry, Chief Inspector, I can't talk about my parishioners any more than a doctor can discuss his patients.'

'That principle surely can't apply when murder is involved. Someone in your village is running around with a poison bottle. Are you really willing to risk another life if you know something?'

'I'm sorry. I did warn you I probably wouldn't be able to help very much.'

Barrett caught Morrissey's eye and raised his eyebrows. Bartholomew was like a shadow boxer, ducking everything that came his way. The difficulty lay in deciding if he were deliberately evasive or innocently unaware.

Morrissey drew back his feet and straightened his jacket. 'I suppose there are very few parishes like this left. Small, compact. Old type vicarage; you must count yourself lucky.'

Bartholomew laughed. 'Once that might have been a good description, but not any more. Shortage of clergy, shortage of money, I'm afraid. There are three parishes combined now: St Jude's, St Mary's in Stenton, and St Anne's in Malminster. As you can see, I get around quite a lot.'

'Same kind of parish problems in all of them?'

'I've no doubt there are if one goes looking.'

'Yes. You'll be carrying the warning round then.' Morrissey got to his feet. 'A good cup of tea,' he said. 'Thanks.' And then: 'Or should I thank Mrs Bartholomew?'

The vicar smiled. 'It's surprising that so many people expect a vicar to be married but accept the celibacy of a Catholic priest. I have no wife, Chief Inspector.'

Barrett put his notebook away, vaguely annoyed there was nothing positive in it, and waited for the chief inspector to move, with Bartholomew, to the door. Instead, Morrissey turned to the butterflies, pinioned silently. While he talked he had been conscious of them filling the long wall, just out of vision but glimpsed when he moved his head. They had disturbed him. Why? Underneath the cassock Bartholomew was a man, and men had strange hobbies.

But wasn't it a small form of evil to take bright life and nail it, wings outstretched?

Bartholomew said from behind his shoulder, 'The better specimens are in the cabinet. Come back when you have more time and I'll let you see them. It's taken many years to build such a collection.'

Barrett asked, half flippantly, 'Bought or caught?'

'Caught. Quite beautiful, aren't they?'

Morrissey thought of the buddleias in his garden and the multi-coloured wings that crowded them in summer; that was where he preferred to see butterflies. He said so.

Bartholomew shrugged. 'To a bird they're a quick snack. These at least had a kind death in the killing jar. Left undisturbed, they'll still be capable of giving pleasure when you and I are rotted, Chief Inspector.'

Morrissey turned away. He said, 'I have a fancy to stay out of my grave for as long as possible.'

'Death,' the vicar reminded him, 'comes like a thief in the night,' and Morrissey smiled sourly.

'And I'm a thief-taker,' he said, and moved towards the door. Bartholomew led them back down the lino-covered passage and apologised again for not being much help. He smiled as they left and Morrissey felt it was more from relief than anything else. Waiting as Barrett closed the gate behind them, he glanced back. Bartholomew was still smiling, and waved a hand as he turned into the vicarage, black cassock flapping.

'What now?' asked Barrett.

'Now we have another chat with Ida Hodge,' said Morrissey. 'And this time, knowing the right questions, we might get some interesting answers.'

Barrett was silent. His thoughts were on a small red-head who had made it plain that next time her husband was away, her door would be open, and he was wondering why the idea had lost its appeal.

SIX

A MOBILE OPERATIONS ROOM had arrived in the Community Centre car park at four-thirty, and there had been a brief flurry of activity establishing a telephone line. At the same time a reporter from the *Malminster Echo* turned up and wandered aimlessly around, waiting to be briefed.

By then a team of police officers were already making house-to-house enquiries, although privately Morrissey thought it wasn't the kind of case where these would prove much help. Each individual enquiry sheet would be fed into the mobile unit's computer for analysis; amazingly faster than old style manual collating, and Morrissey approved. He approved too of the operations room as a place to think, to put his feet up, and to get a good cup of coffee. Although that couldn't happen until they had seen Ida Hodge again.

Barrett, he knew, would be less concerned with tea and putting his feet up than with ogling WPC Janet Yarby, who fed the computer. His sergeant had been trying for nearly a year, but without much success, to persuade her his randy reputation wasn't deserved. And she still refused to go out with him.

Morrissey thought he knew where his sergeant's libido was itching and grinned to himself. Janet had other things on her mind, like moving across to CID, and he didn't think Barrett had a hope in hell. Not that he intended telling him. With Janet around, Barrett would be on his toes, hoping to impress.

On Church Row, Betty Hartley's cottage was locked up and quiet, the local constable returned to normal duties. Strange how little impact violent death left on its surroundings. A painstaking search of belongings hadn't thrown any light on her death or revealed any clue to family; which left them still not knowing where to find her relatives. If she had any. That was something else he needed to bring up with Ida Hodge. Even the dead woman's medical records showed only a blank space where next of kin should be.

He wondered how many mourners would turn out for the funeral. Not many, he guessed.

Once, he had stood with a bleak east wind blowing through a cemetery while a coffin was lowered, and no one else there but his sergeant, the preacher, and a representative from the local council. It was a scene frozen uncomfortably in his mind.

When he stepped into Ida's kitchen her husband was there, and his presence seemed to curb his wife's tongue, stopping it running off into trivial streams of gossip. Because of that Morrissey did something he wouldn't normally do, and let Edwin Hodge stay in the room while his wife was questioned.

When he asked about next of kin, Ida said sharply, 'She'd got insurance, you know; there's no need hunting anybody to fork out. Betty expected she'd have to put herself away when the time came. Couldn't rely on that sniffy son of hers in Brinckly. Didn't want him bothered anyway. Never came near. Never once. Prudential, them's who you want. Here, I've got his address.' She rooted in a kitchen drawer and came out with a piece of paper.

'Her son?' said Morrissey as Barrett took it to copy the address.

'Insurance man.'

Her husband said, 'It's her son's address he's asked you for, why don't you give it him?' Ida remained stubborn. 'Give it out,' Edwin ordered, 'there's other things.' Sullenly, his wife went back to the drawer.

'It'll be a waste of time,' said Ida as she handed another bit of paper to Barrett. 'There's a husband, but God only knows where he's gone. Anyway, her Willie might not be there now, it's years since she gave me that.'

Morrissey remembered a psychology lecture he had attended a year or so ago. 'The root of gossip is loneliness; it allows a vicarious participation in the life from which the gossiper feels excluded, and sometimes goes deeper, providing a way of avenging past hurts.' The lecturer had looked young, unworldly, and Morrissey had taken everything with a pinch of salt; but now, if he linked the words to Betty Hartley, they didn't seem that naïve. Someone would have to go to

Brinckly, and soon, to find out if the son still lived
there.

'Are you calling it suicide then?' Edwin asked.

Morrissey said, 'It's a strong probability.'

'Never,' said Ida, 'it's that Marion Walsh what
should be dead, told you that before when you said it
was her milk.'

'I didn't say the milk had come from Mrs Walsh,'
Morrissey corrected. 'You made the assumption.'

'Weren't no assumption,' Ida told him. 'It had to
come from her, it didn't come from my Ned.' Her
husband backed her up.

'S'right,' he agreed. 'Never got no gold top from
me.'

'You want to ask that Mrs Goddard about it—her
husband and Marion Walsh was having it off. Dead
queer she was this morning when she come in the
shop; looked like a warmed-up zombie. Then me and
Betty seen her a bit later, coming away from that
Walsh house. Now what had she been up to there, eh?
That's what me and Betty wondered.'

Barrett's eyes lit up; it was all coming together. The
whole thing might be sewn up tonight.

Morrissey had the same thought, but in his case
there was disquiet too. He didn't like it when things
looked too easy; it usually meant they turned out to
be wrong. But perhaps this would be the exception
that proved the rule, because when Ida stopped talking he had been given a complete picture of motive
and opportunity. He came away armed with Helen

Goddard's address, and the knowledge that there were a lot of questions for her to answer.

'Search warrant?' Barrett asked when they were outside.

'I think we must, not that anyone with sense would leave cyanide lying around. We'll take the car and pick up Janet Yarby on the way; we need a WPC with us.'

He waited for his sergeant to react to her name, but Barrett, whose mind was still firmly fixed on the red-head in Malminster and his chances of getting caught, simply started the car and moved it away from the kerb. At his side Morrissey was momentarily non-plussed. Had Barrett given up the chase? Not possible.

He excluded Barrett's personal life from his thoughts and concentrated instead on what he would say to Helen Goddard. He never felt completely at ease when the major suspect in a case was a woman. He tended perhaps to take a too-kindly view of the opposite sex. His daughter, now in her late teens, would call that sexist, and think it an insult.

Janet Yarby was glad to take a break from the computer keyboard. 'What sort of woman is she?' the WPC enquired, getting into the car. Morrissey shook his head. He had a mental picture of Marion Walsh and wondered if Helen Goddard was the same type. But when he rang the bell at the Goddard house, and she opened the door to them, he recognised she was not; the two women were opposite ends of the spectrum. This woman's intelligent hazel eyes watched him silently, and reminded him of his wife. There was the same firmness of chin, the same high cheek-bones, the same air of quiet containment; but the hair was different. Helen Goddard's ash-brown had been tamed and fastened high on her head, while Margaret's was darker and shorter. For some reason recognition of that difference came as a relief.

When the police car had crunched to a stop outside the house Helen had been in her bedroom. She already knew by then that part, at least, of what Marion Walsh had told her was true. Betty Hartley was dead, and the village was full of policemen. Now something else was true, they were here, about to enter her home, and she wasn't sure she could cope with much more. She wished Robert would come home. She wished the day could be carefully unravelled like a piece of knitting, pulled back to that morning and knitted up again differently.

Her pallor and dark-circled eyes warned Morrissey she mustn't be pushed too far. He would have liked to avoid what had to come, as he followed her into the sitting-room and watched her seat herself quietly on a straight-backed chair and wait. The soft blue sweater gave her skin a kind of translucence, and he found himself studying her face. Instinctively he knew it would be hard for her to hide anything. He wondered again at the similarity to his wife and he wondered too about Robert Goddard, about the type of

sexuality that would send him from this woman to
Marion Walsh.

Morrissey's eyes moved unthinking from the wide
forehead to the generous mouth and a faint pink came
on to Helen Goddard's cheekbones. The chief inspector moved his eyes away deliberately to take in the
room and contrast it with the Walsh woman's designer style. Here there was obvious good taste, hap-
hazard perhaps, things chosen impulsively because
they were liked, but they told him a lot about Helen
Goddard; hers was a chintzy room, a room to come
home to and feel safe in. Against the light from the
bay window, a blue bowl held daffodils and reflected
in the dark polished top of a small rosewood desk. A
tall bookcase in the same wood was packed to over-
flowing, and photographs, some in silver frames some
in wood, stood on almost every flat surface. And
what of her husband Morrissey thought, what was
there of him in this room? He cleared his throat and
sat on the settee, knowing that doing so would make
her feel more comfortable.

Janet Yarby approved the gentle approach, and
smiled at Barrett's scowl.

Morrissey said, 'What time will your husband be
home, Mrs Goddard?'

'I think about six-thirty.'

'Do you know why we're here?'

She shook her head; her hands were in her lap,
small and slim, and she kept her eyes fixed on them.
'I know something is going on in the village, I heard

that Betty Hartley had died. But no, I don't know what it has to do with me.'

'Do you know Marion Walsh?'

Her hands curled around each other tightly and for a minute he thought she wasn't going to answer, then she let them go slack again and said, 'Yes, I've met her.'

'Is she a friend?'

'No!'

'I want you to tell me exactly what you have done today since you got up this morning. Will you do that?'

'I made breakfast,' Helen said obediently. 'Then I went to the post office to buy stamps. Betty Hartley was there waiting for bread, and Ida Hodge the milkman's wife. They were talking.'

'Do you know what they were talking about?'

'Me,' she said. 'They were talking about me.' For the first time she looked at him directly and there was defiance and pain in her dark eyes. 'My husband has been having an affair with Marion Walsh. That's what they were talking about.'

'And when you came out of the shop, where did you go then?' he asked gently.

'I walked up Hill Road. I remember the church clock struck nine.'

'Did you go into the Walsh house?'

Helen frowned. 'I think I did. I rang the bell but no one came.'

'Why did you go?'

'I don't know. I wanted to see her. I wanted to tell her to leave Robert alone.'

'But you didn't see her?'

'No.'

'Did you touch anything?'

'The gate. The doorbell. I think...' she frowned again. 'I think I touched a milk bottle. I had some absurd idea of emptying it over her head.'

It was an action Morrissey accepted would be more in keeping with her character than administering poison. But poison had been administered. 'What then?' he prompted, and heard about the Trumpton seat and her last sight of Betty, and the hurried walk home to collect her library books.

'What type of books do you enjoy?' he asked.

She looked at him and smiled mirthlessly. 'I chose three murder mysteries. I suppose that seems appropriate?'

'I don't think I mentioned murder,' he said.

'But Marion Walsh has.' And she told him about the other woman's visit. Everything, except what had been said about Robert, and ended, 'Was it the truth, had her milk been poisoned?'

There was no longer any point in stepping gently. 'Yes, it had, and unfortunately Betty Hartley took that particular bottle home with her.'

Helen sighed, a small, empty sound. 'I wished her dead, but I didn't put poison in her milk.'

'We have to search your house, Mrs Goddard. A
warrant will be here soon, but if you don't object it
would save time to start now.'

'Do whatever you need to,' she shrugged. 'It
doesn't really seem to matter any more.'

Janet Yarby met his eyes and he nodded. He told
Helen, 'The WPC will stay in here with you, and if
you twist her arm she makes a decent cup of tea.'

Helen shook her head.

At the top of the stairs, carpeted, like the hall, in
plain green Wilton, a small room on the left had been
converted into a professional, well equipped dark-
room. With a sinking stomach Morrissey knew that
its being there brought Helen Goddard one step
nearer to guilt. He had a reluctance to look in the
cupboard where the chemicals were kept, but when he
did the bottle was clearly labelled on the third shelf.
Cyanide of Potassium.

'Bag it,' he said heavily, and turned away. He saw
Barrett's satisfaction. That's what he should feel too.
The cardinal rule in police work was not to get personally involved. He had now to go downstairs and
tell Helen Goddard what they had found and after
that things would take their course. The drive to
Malminster, the formal statement, the decision of
whether or not to charge her there and then. But the
final decision wouldn't be solely his, and for that he
was grateful.

WPC Yarby stood up as they went into the downstairs room. Helen Goddard looked at their faces and

then at the polythene bag Barrett was carrying. She shook her head.

'I shall need you to come to the police station and make a statement,' Morrissey said formally. 'If you would like a solicitor...' He thought she was going to faint, and both he and Janet Yarby moved towards her, but she gripped the sides of her chair tightly and forced her head up.

'I'd like to wait a few minutes longer until my husband comes home,' she said. 'If that would be all right? I want him to know where I am.'

'The WPC will go with you to get your coat,' he said expressionlessly, and stood silently until they were out of the room.

'I don't get it,' Barrett blurted. 'You're holding back and it seems open and shut. Jealous wife, poison handy...'

'And still a lot of ends to tie up. Fingerprints to check, chemical analysis. It's all circumstantial up to now. We don't know yet if that stuff matches whatever was in the milk.'

'We know it's cyanide.'

'We don't know it's that particular compound,' Morrissey said, 'and we don't know why Helen Goddard left it there to be found after the Walsh woman had warned her.' He heard a key turn in the outside door and moved into the hall.

'What in hell's name is going on!' Goddard snapped, coming in and seeing his wife on the stairs, wearing her outdoor coat with WPC Yarby at her side. 'Helen? What's been happening?'

'They think I tried to kill Marion Walsh,' she said unsteadily, and Morrissey shook his head at Barrett, gratified at the speed the unspoken command was picked up and Helen Goddard taken out to the waiting car before she could say anything else.

'It's bloody ridiculous,' said Goddard in anger. 'Helen would be incapable.' But Morrissey saw fear in the man's eyes and reflected that he too had equal access to the cyanide.

He told Goddard stonily, 'Mrs Goddard has agreed to come to the police station and make a statement, and I have to tell you now that we shall require one from you too.'

'Not until I've spoken to my solicitor,' Goddard said, moving towards the telephone. 'Not until then.'

SEVEN

THERE WAS A steady drizzle of rain and the village street was empty except for the vicar, out under his black umbrella. Morrissey, sitting in the front of the police car, noted him. Robert Goddard was still at home trying to contact his solicitor, and would drive himself, an odd decision and one that said a lot about his marriage. In the same circumstances Morrissey would have been glued to Margaret's side; only at the station would he have exercised his right to one telephone call. But since marriage counselling wasn't his business, and his prime interest lay in Helen Goddard not her husband, it would be politic to take her statement now if she were willing, before any complications were introduced.

He was in a sombre frame of mind when they entered the divisional headquarters; sometimes, rarely, he would have exchanged jobs with anybody, and that feeling was creeping over him now. He left Barrett at the desk to wait for Robert Goddard, ignoring the sergeant's palpable resentment, which was something Morrissey could live with. There would be distraction enough with himself and a WPC in the interview room, without a third and wholly hostile presence.

Barrett would have argued that his chief was treating Helen as a witness and not a suspect, and Morrissey couldn't rationalise his instinct to go easy. He dismissed the idea that her faint but unmistakable resemblance to Margaret had anything to do with it. Such an airy-fairy notion as a sixth sense was an embarrassment; but there was no better way to describe his occasional hunches.

He gave Helen a little time to grow used to the bare room before he turned on the tape recorder. And he offered her the choice of waiting for a solicitor.

'I don't see the point,' she said bleakly. 'I'd rather get the whole thing over with.' He thought she had been going to add 'and go home', but if so she left the words unsaid and he let the familiar process begin.

Her voice went on without hesitation, repeating what she had already told him, adding only small things; the vicar crossing the road, her dislike of the allotment path, the blue car that had blocked its exit onto Vicarage Lane and snagged her tights as she pushed by.

'Is that it?' she asked when he finally stopped the tape.

'When it's been typed up and you've read and signed it; and when we've taken your fingerprints. Who did the blue car belong to?'

'I don't know. I supposed my neighbour had a visitor. I haven't noticed it in the lane before.'

'That would be Mr . . . ?'

'Sutcliffe. Brian Sutcliffe. Of course it could have belonged to someone on the allotments. It was higher up than his house.'

'Did you notice the make?'

'A Volvo, dark blue. Does it matter?'

'In a murder inquiry anything might matter.'

'Yes.' She half raised her hands then let them fall. 'I can't believe any of this. All I could think this morning was how terrible it felt to be losing Robert, and now . . . now I don't think I want to live with him at all.'

'Marion Walsh?'

'Everything felt dirty; the house, me. I know it's ridiculous but I've showered three times since she came this afternoon, and I still feel soiled.'

Morrissey squinted at the WPC who had taken over from Janet Yarby. 'See if you can rustle up some tea,' he said. 'Tell Pace I want it in a hurry.' She moved from her chair and he looked again at Helen, feeling a faint stirring at the back of his mind, a quickening of interest not wholly professional. Barrett wouldn't have found that a problem, but Barrett still had a lot to learn.

She said bleakly, 'I want someone to tell me Marion was lying, and there's something worth saving.'

He couldn't give her that reassurance.

The shadows around her eyes seemed larger than ever and she was staring at him intently. When the question came it rocked him, although he knew it was an attempt to make sense of what had happened to her.

'You must be Robert's age. Tell me about Marion Walsh. When you talked to her were you thinking it would be good to take her to bed?'

He felt shock. Not at the nature of the question, but because it probed beneath the shell of chief inspector, and reached the man. It made him remember the way light had passed through Marion Walsh's thin robe.

From the corner of his eye he saw the WPC struggle with her face as she sat on her chair. If she grinned, he thought, he'd see she'd have a month on traffic duty.

Then Helen Goddard said, 'I'm sorry, that was stupid,' and took away any need to answer.

PC Pace brought a tray of tea and a message from Barrett that Robert Goddard and his solicitor were at the desk demanding to see his wife. Morrissey set the least objectionable mug in front of Helen and lifted his eyebrows.

She shook her head. 'I don't want to see either of them. If you charge me, then I might need a solicitor. But not until then.'

She said nothing more after that, content to sip strong tea until her statement came back for signing, and when that happened read it quickly and signed without question.

She passed it back to Morrissey. 'Chief Inspector, do you enjoy your work?' It wasn't an idle question, she genuinely wondered if there could be anything enjoyable in it.

For a second time she surprised him.

'I have to, otherwise I wouldn't be any use in the job.' This time the answer had been easy, and he didn't need to admit the same question sometimes slid of its own volition into his mind. At those times the answer never came so easily. It could happen again now if he had to send this woman down to the cells. 'Someone has to keep peace, catch burglars...'

'Discover why Betty Hartley died.'

'A mistake,' he said. 'The poison was meant for Marion Walsh, wasn't it?' He kept his eyes fixed on the statement that lay on the table before him, while his ears listened for an unthinking answer. An incriminating answer?

Instead she said, 'I had a daily when the children were small. We had a cup of coffee together every morning.'

An old saying slipped into his mind. Two birds with one stone. Poison a bottle of milk and where was the guarantee it would reach only one person? So far they'd been making assumptions. Start thinking laterally and it was a different landscape.

'I hadn't any reason to poison Betty. I'd no more secrets to keep.' She rested her elbows on the table and her shoulders slumped. 'I'm very tired,' she said. 'Can I go home soon?'

If he went by the book he should keep her here, but instinct still insisted she was just part of the background. The person he wanted remained out of focus, and the heavy gut feeling that the motive for murder stemmed from something much worse than adultery stayed with him. Morrissey chose not to go by the book.

'As soon as we have your fingerprints I'll have a car take you home,' he said, and part of him felt lighter for having said it.

When he had seen her down the corridor, the WPC at her side, and made doubly sure the police car taking her home would be unmarked, he went back to wait for Robert Goddard and his solicitor to take her place. No more secrets, Helen Goddard had said. For the first time he wondered where Marion Walsh's money came from. A heavily insured husband? It was a question to pursue tomorrow and he filed it in his mind. In the meantime he fully intended to give Goddard an uncomfortable ride, and the longer he could make it last, the more breathing space it would give his wife. He heard Barrett's voice and put on his most intimidating face.

It would be interesting to see if Goddard would squirm.

EIGHT

MORRISSEY LIVED ON the north side of Malminster, where the ground level was higher than the rest of the town. They had bought the semi-detached house in the quiet cul-de-sac when Katie was born, and Margaret's one fear since then had been that he might be transferred. But he'd been lucky, moving steadily upwards through CID. Their 1930s semi was solidly built with mullioned bays, and a garden large enough to keep them both busy. Over the years, Malminster itself had grown and, with local government reorganisation, had eaten up smaller districts. He had watched the value of his home increase so dramatically that now it seemed impossible the figures on his house insurance policy had anything to do with reality.

On the morning after Betty Hartley's death Morrissey was up early. Margaret had half woken as he slid out of bed, and he had taken his clothes into the bathroom so as not to disturb her more. Rising an hour or so before the alarm stirred the rest of his family had become a habit when he needed some thinking time.

It was chill and fresh after overnight rain, and a small shower of droplets fell on his head when he opened the greenhouse door. Underneath the standings, seedlings were thrusting out of seed trays, begging to be potted on. As his fingers worked the soft loam his concentration was given to Betty Hartley's death.

He had half accepted that without the daily help's light-fingeredness, Marion Walsh would have been the victim. But there were other possibilities; the cyanide could have been intended for both women, and if that were so then the poisoner had a motive common to both.

There was the possibility too that the bottle on Betty's table could have been rigged after she was dead—dangerous perhaps for whoever was responsible, but not impossible—and it neatly offered the Walsh woman as a red-herring. It could explain why the milk taken from Marion Walsh's fridge had been untainted. The lab report last night had been a surprise; he had been almost a hundred per cent certain both bottles had been tampered with.

Another thought came and stayed his fingers. Marion Walsh hadn't shown either the fear or surprise he had expected when faced with the reality of an attempt on her life. Why? Because she had automatically put Helen Goddard in the guilty seat? And why, in that case, had she warned her rival to get rid of the cyanide?

Because she didn't want there to be proof she was the target and be put firmly at the centre of police attention. And that meant Mrs Walsh must have secrets of her own.

In that case would she have deliberately kept back a suspect pint of milk? He put himself mentally into her kitchen; her body blocking the inside of the refrigerator from his view. From Barrett's too?

He cursed and dusted the peaty compost from his fingers. Neil Barrett wouldn't be pleased to be woken up and told Marion Walsh's dustbin had to be searched. Too bad. He went back to the house and dialled the sergeant's home, and as he listened to the tone ringing out, wondered wickedly if Barrett was alone.

BREAKFAST HAD BECOME a sort of ritual replacement for dinner; the only meal Morrissey and his family ate together with any regularity. It was a fact of life Margaret had learned to live with, that the higher up the ladder he climbed, the less he kept regular hours. He looked at his daughter and tried to imagine her in ten years' time. When Margaret had been that age, it had been flower-power, long hair and loons, Bob Dylan. Now it was Goths, and his arts student daughter looked like an animated corpse in pallid make-up and purple fingernails.

'Mildred Snow rang last night,' Margaret said, intuitively diverting fatherly fears. 'She wanted me to ask you what had been happening in Little Henge; apparently her sister lives there and saw you coming out of the vicarage.'

'It's possible,' said Morrissey, who made it a rule not to talk about cases he was working on.

'I told her you wouldn't discuss it,' Margaret said calmly. He looked at her suspiciously. 'She didn't believe me, of course. But whatever it is I expect I shall find out from the local paper on Friday.'

He grunted. 'All it will say is that a woman was found dead in her home, and the police are treating her death as suspicious.'

'You mean she got bumped off,' said his son, and then displayed an average thirteen-year-old's liking for gore. 'Was it a knife? Blood all over like *Psycho*?'

'It was not,' Morrissey snapped. 'And I'll thank you not to go spreading it round your school.'

'What's the good of having a top cop for a father if you never get to know anything juicy?'

Margaret got Morrissey's ''now look what you've started'' scowl and told Michael, 'Shut up and eat your breakfast.'

'But Mum!'

'Eat.' She looked at her husband. 'It's no good trying to intimidate me,' she said, 'I know you too well.'

'The vicar offered us tea.' Morrissey made truth serve his own purpose. 'That's why we were coming out of the vicarage. Though what it has to do with Mildred Snow I can't imagine.'

'He's her vicar too,' Margaret said. 'At St Anne's.'

Three parishes, Bartholomew had said. Little Henge, St Anne's and Stenton.

'Phil Duffin went there,' Michael offered. 'You know, he did a runner last year. Used to get his leg pulled for being a choirboy.'

Margaret remembered when the boy had gone missing; it had made her keep a closer watch on Michael for a long time. Then, as things do, it had slipped to the back of her mind and she had relaxed. Now, worrying again, she said, 'Wasn't he ever found?'

Her son was unconcerned. 'Dunno. Didn't come back to Fisher Comp.'

Katie contributed succinctly, 'I expect he's renting somewhere.' She enjoyed airing things her parents would rather she didn't know, and her father's warning look did no good. 'No point looking like that, Dad. Mike knows all about that sort of thing.'

His son and daughter grinned at each other. Had it been like this for his parents, Morrissey wondered, this constant feeling of sitting on a time-bomb? 'Do you know what happened to the Duffin boy, John?' he heard his wife ask. But it hadn't been his case, and he hadn't thought about it for over a year.

THERE WOULD BE no purpose served in calling at the office; whatever messages had come would be duplicated and waiting for him at Little Henge, and so he drove straight to the village. Barrett was already there, yawning resentfully.

'Shouldn't stay up late,' said Morrissey unsym-
pathetically. 'Any luck with the bin?'

'Four from outside, and one in the pedal bin. Mrs
Walsh is not amused.'

'I didn't expect her to be,' said Morrissey. 'She'll be
even less amused before the day is up.'

Organising house-to-house enquiries had fallen to
a man Morrissey had always found likeable. He had
been pleased to hear that Alan Blake had got his promotion to inspector. Less pleased, he suspected,
would be Neil Barrett. Until the local investigation
wound up, Blake would be based at the incident room
with Janet Yarby. *And* he was unattached. Certain
areas of life seemed not to be going too well for Barrett. Morrissey asked, in hope more than expecta-
tion, 'Anything much happening, Alan?'

Blake pulled a face and shook his head. 'Not a lot,
except for the consistency that no one seems to have
anything good to say about the Hartley woman. It's
surprising how many people she rubbed up the wrong
way.'

'I'd like to have a look at the reports from Vicarage Lane if you've got them in, particularly from the
Sutcliffe house. I'm interested in a blue Volvo parked
near there yesterday morning.'

'Mm. Should be here. Yep, Bartholomew, Goddard, Sutcliffe and Bellinger.'

Sutcliffe, Morrissey saw, hadn't been at home;
neither had his wife. But, like Marion Walsh, they
had a daily: unfortunately theirs didn't gossip and

there was nothing fruitful in her statement. But the Bellinger report was more hopeful. A retired accountant, he'd been less interested in talking about Betty Hartley than in complaining about a Volvo that had scraped his bumper as he backed out of his drive. Mr Bellinger had been very irate; the thought that it was he who had been at fault in reversing into the road obviously hadn't entered his head.

'How would you feel about setting up again, Alan?' Morrissey said. 'Different lot of questions.' He waited for a protest but it didn't come.

'Your case,' Blake said, his eyes on Janet's bent head. 'Whatever you need.' Morrissey was glad to see Barrett glowering; it restored his faith.

'I want to know about strangers, especially near the Walsh house. Not just yesterday; anytime in the last three months. If anyone comments on Marion Walsh's comings and goings, encourage them. The other thing is this dark blue Volvo, parked near the allotment path on Vicarage Lane yesterday morning. And something else you could do for me; find out the registration number on the Walsh car and run it through records. Any previous addresses on file would be a help.'

'That it?'

'For now. Any messages come through?'

Blake opened a folder and passed over its contents. Two lab reports, preliminary post-mortem report, fingerprint report. The first three the chief inspector had seen the previous evening, but the fourth was new. Helen Goddard's fingerprints had been found on the Walsh gate and the back door. Not on the milk bottle though; that had held only Betty Hartley's. At some point then, it had been wiped clean; had to have been if not even the milkman's prints were there. The good news was that the only prints on the cyanide of potassium taken from the dark-room were Robert Goddard's; Helen's were absent. But should he regard that as good or a setback?

'Be funny if it turned out to be him after all,' Barrett said as he pulled neatly into the kerb on Vicarage Lane. 'Here we are, running around in circles, following hares, just because it looks too easy.'

'Is that a genuine opinion or sour grapes?' Morrissey asked.

'Sour grapes. Think the gap in the hedge over there is Bellinger's drive? Bit risky reversing out if it is; no vision at all until he's stuck right across the road.'

'Then I should point that out while you're there,' Morrissey said gently. 'Come across to the Goddard house when you're finished.'

Helen opened the door to him, still pale but less uncertain. 'Chief Inspector. Are there more questions, or have you come to arrest me?' Her eyes were still direct.

'Questions.'

'Then you'd better come in. Can I offer you coffee, or wouldn't you feel safe?'

'I'd feel safe, but I won't have any. Is your husband here?'

'At the office I should think, I don't really know. For the first time since we married I didn't make breakfast for him. I think it was rather a shock.'

'Is it going to be permanent?'

'I'm not sure.' She led him into the sitting-room, and lit the gas fire. 'I find it chilly today, but whether it's real or imaginary I don't know.'

He sat on the edge of the settee and watched the glow of heat on her face. 'This may be painful,' he said. 'But I want you to tell me everything you know about Marion Walsh. More than that perhaps; anything you've heard or guessed too.'

She looked at him. 'Are you asking if she had other men besides Robert?' Her voice was so matter of fact Morrissey wondered at it. 'Don't be embarrassed, Chief Inspector, yesterday I had all the shame I could hold. Today I'm anaesthetised. I'd like you to see something.' She got up and went out of the room. Morrissey followed. Up the stairs and into a large double bedroom, cool in white and green.

'That's Marion Walsh's bedroom,' she said, staring through the window.

Morrissey looked down the length of garden at the green roofed house. His eyes could make out vague furniture shapes in the upper room, but nothing distinct.

'You need these, Chief Inspector,' she said, and handed him the field glasses. 'I shan't use them again, I've nothing left to be jealous of.'

He took them, stared at her.

'You're shocked. I suppose technically I've been committing an offence. A Peeping Tom. But you see, Chief Inspector, I probably know even more than poor Betty about Marion Walsh's lovers, and that's what you want, isn't it?'

NINE

'I'M NOT GOING TO say they were her lovers because I don't know that. I was a jealous wife, not a voyeur.' Helen Goddard was writing as she spoke. But she had already made that claim and Morrissey was lost for a reply. It was one thing to protest, as he had on many occasions, that policemen were human; quite a different thing to be reminded of it so sharply. A wave of contempt for Robert Goddard washed over him and he knew it was illogical. Goddard's infidelity had been no worse, less even, than a hundred other men Morrissey had come across during his career; the difference lay in Helen Goddard. It was against his own rules to lay a mantle of innocence on her shoulders; it took two to make a quarrel, two to breed infidelity.

She held out the sheet of blue notepaper and he took it without speaking. He recognised the three names; one surprised him. The most obvious thing they had in common was money. Was that how Marion Walsh kept up her lifestyle? A string of grateful studs.

'You must have been surprised,' he said, 'when . . . er . . .'

'When I saw the company Robert kept,' Helen said wryly. 'A bit grateful too that I wasn't the only fool around. But at least their wives didn't have it rubbed in their faces. There's an old saying about not fouling your own doorstep, isn't there, Chief Inspector? Robert should have respected that.'

'Would it have made it better?'

'Less painful perhaps. It would have allowed me the luxury of uncertainty.' She saw him frown at the paper and knew what bothered him. 'They don't live in the village,' she said, 'and you're wondering how I recognised them. It's quite easy; all of them are members of the Chamber of Commerce in Malminster like Robert. I've met them and their wives at different times. Occasionally Emily Turner and I meet up for a coffee.'

'But you haven't told her?'

Helen shook her head. 'Would you?' she asked simply. 'Given the same circumstances, would you?'

It was a question he took back to the car with him. Would he, given similar circumstances, tell a fellow officer he was being cuckolded? Barrett came out of the Bellinger drive and crossed the road, grinning. 'Number and a fair description of the driver,' he said getting into the car.

Morrissey got in the other side and laid out the theoretical question of cuckolding. Would Neil tell or not tell? he asked.

Barrett felt his bowels grow hot as he thought of David Pace's wife. He gripped the wheel and stared up the hill, quite unable to look at Morrissey, wondering how he'd been found out.

The chief inspector leaned back thoughtfully. He knew his sergeant, and he knew he'd touched a raw nerve; the question was—before or after the act?

'Good job we policemen don't go in for that sort of thing,' he said carefully, 'all the pretty wives around. Bad for station morale, not to mention the sackings.'

'Yes, sir.' Barrett started the engine. 'What now, sir?'

'Now that we both know more than we did a few minutes ago, we'll have a talk with Marion Walsh,' Morrissey said, and as Barrett turned the car added, 'Give you time to think up an answer.'

From the way she was dressed, Morrissey guessed Marion Walsh had been about to go out. She looked expensive in silky beige and her glance at Barrett was cold.

'Oh, it's you again. What is it this time, bins or drains?'

Morrissey put his hand on the door and pushed. 'Considering the threat to your life, you seem remarkably unconcerned and uncooperative, Mrs Walsh. Now why would that be?'

She had backed away as he came into the kitchen; now she folded her arms and stared at him. 'I told you yesterday it was a mistake. There's no danger at all.'

'You did something else yesterday too; you tried to intimidate a witness. Mrs Goddard told us about your visit, and about her husband's relationship with you.'

'Stupid bitch!'

'If you really believed Mrs Goddard had caused Betty Hartley's death, you had a moral duty to tell the police.'

'Morality doesn't come into it, and neither does duty, so don't preach at me, Inspector. I called on Helen Goddard to tell her I wouldn't be seeing her husband again. And that's all. Anything else she told you is from her own imagination and her word against mine.'

Her demotion of him had been deliberate. Morrissey was sure of that as he said calmly, 'Mrs Goddard doesn't centre in our enquiries. Someone else is out there, Mrs Walsh, and that someone seems to want you dead.'

Barrett looked surprised by Morrissey's bluntness. His chief's face was stone, showing neither sympathy nor concern for the woman before him, and the only reaction she gave was a slight widening of her eyes, and an abrupt turning on her heel as she went into the sitting-room and lit a cigarette.

'Trying to frighten me, Inspector?'

'Chief Inspector.'

'Of course; as in firemen. Is there any fire in you, Inspector, or has it all been long since put out?' She exhaled smoke through her nostrils, reversing the role of dragon and maiden. Barrett wondered what it would take for Morrissey to break through her composure.

'Who might want you to die, Mrs Walsh? Not a jealous wife; in these days she'd be more likely to go for a quick divorce and half his money. So it must be something else. What?'

'Why don't you look for whoever wanted to kill Betty instead, because, quite frankly, you're beginning to bore me. In fact I'm not sure your continual presence couldn't be called harassment.' She strolled to the small table between the two windows. 'Shall I call your chief constable and find out?'

'Why not ring Bernard Moxon instead?'

Her hand hesitated and withdrew. 'Bernard Moxon?'

'Yes. You do know him, I believe.'

'Doesn't everyone?'

'Not in the same way. But as the chief constable's brother-in-law he should be sympathetic.'

'What exactly does that mean?'

'I believe Philip Turner and Martin Cotton are friends of yours too.'

Now she was rattled. Barrett felt a sneaking admiration for Morrissey. In days to come, he thought, when he'd reached the same rank, he'd look back and remember this.

'You really have been concentrating on your homework.' Marion stubbed out the cigarette and lit another. 'Men find me attractive; should that give me cause to complain?'

'Mrs Walsh, either you've made a bad enemy since you came here, or you made one before. That isn't supposition—I have a dead woman to prove it.'

'I don't believe . . .'

'Did Mrs Hartley usually have a cup of coffee with you?'

'Yes, but . . .'

'What did she know about you and your life that would make someone want both of you to be silent?'

'Nothing! Nothing, damn you!' The words were almost a screech. Ash dropped from her cigarette onto the carpet and she rubbed it in with her toe. 'Middle-aged men like yourself, *Chief* Inspector, like a little excitement.'

'Do they pay for it?' Morrissey said bluntly.

'Gifts of appreciation aren't illegal. None of them would have a reason to harm me.'

'But somebody has. I'd like a list of all your male callers. I promise our enquiries will be very discreet.'

'I'm not sure discretion is a part of your nature,' she said. 'Let me see, the milkman calls each day, the postman too, the vicar pops in occasionally. I had a man round to clear the drains a week ago. And then of course there's you. If there's nothing else, nothing important, I was about to go out.'

'Where did you live before you came here?'

'None of your damn business.'

'Then why did you move to Little Henge, Mrs Walsh?' Morrissey said softly. 'What was the attraction, or should I say *who*?'

'Nothing and no one; it was simply a bad mistake.' She looked at her watch. 'And if you want to know where I'm going now, I'd be delighted to tell you. Scissors. Very good hairdressers, you should recommend them to your wife.' She put out her second cigarette and looked at him.

Morrissey said, 'I think there will be another attempt on your life, and soon. Keep that in mind, won't you?' and walked out of the room.

Barrett stayed silent until they were in the car, then he said, 'Was that to worry her, or did you mean it?'

'I meant it,' Morrissey said heavily. 'Somewhere near Little Henge is someone frightened enough to kill. And if we don't manage to break through Marion Walsh's defences soon, he'll do it.'

'He?'

'Whatever,' Morrissey said. 'Makes no difference.'

There was a pot of coffee hot and ready at the MOR, and a message for Morrissey. He read it while Barrett hung over Janet Yarby and watched her quick fingers feed the Volvo registration into the computer.

Of the foil caps retrieved from Marion's rubbish, one showed a perforation the same diameter as that in Betty's kitchen; it was the cap from the pedal bin, and that alone had been rinsed clean, the others still had traces of cream on them. Marion had knowingly intended to mislead them. One thing was for sure— she certainly wasn't going to tell them why in a hurry.

Morrissey was uncomfortably aware that his interviews with her were becoming a clash of wills, and he didn't like it. He could threaten her with a charge of obstruction, but unless he was prepared to carry it out it would simply wrong-foot him, and it wouldn't get him anywhere. Of course he could take her into Malminster and question her in one of the small bare rooms where Helen Goddard had made her statement, but he didn't think that would produce anything either.

He sat down to drink his coffee. If they could go backwards into her life, get another address . . . Then Morrissey suddenly saw how to do it and scalded his mouth into the bargain. He took it out on Barrett.

'If you can tear yourself away, Neil, there's things to do.'

Barrett thought his stomach wouldn't last much longer; first no breakfast and now no coffee. It rumbled to prove the point. Janet laughed at him and reached into her shoulder bag. 'Here,' she fished out a Mars bar. 'Eat it before you frighten the natives.'

He brightened. 'Dinner next week by way of thanks?'

She shook her head. 'Nice try. Just a replacement on my desk sometime.'

Morrissey gave her an approving smile and went out. 'You've got some telephoning to do,' he told Barrett when they were outside. 'Take the car back; I'll have to bring my own. When you get to the office I want to know which estate agent handled the sale of the Walsh house, and when you find out, I want the file on it. Don't take any arguments, make sure they know it's important.'

Barrett was approving. 'And you'll have her solicitor, her bank, her old address . . . Why didn't I think of that?'

'Because I'm the chief inspector and you're learning,' Morrissey said complacently.

The glow of having had a good idea stayed with him until they drew into the police yard together and went upstairs.

His office door was open.

'Put it back!' he roared, his arms and legs appearing to grow extra inches as he stretched them across the doorway. Barrett squinted past and saw the cinnamon chair smugly behind Morrissey's desk, while the old one hung uncertainly between the two men from supplies.

'Orders is,' one of them tried, 'this 'ere's redundant.'

'Not half as redundant as you'll be if you don't put it back,' Morrissey threatened.

For a moment there was an impasse, then the second man said resignedly, 'Put it back, Sam, it'll have to wait.'

Morrissey lowered his arms until his comfort symbol was back in place. Sam shunted the cinnamon chair into the far corner.

'Oh no, you don't,' the chief inspector said. 'Out with it; take it home for the kids, drop it out of the window, burn the bloody thing, but don't let me see it again.'

When it had gone he lowered his buttocks onto the old black leather with a sigh. 'There's a lot to be said for diplomacy,' he said, 'but sometimes intimidation works a hell of a sight better.'

'HEARTHSTONE PROPERTIES,' said Barrett, 'owned by a Martin Cotton. Isn't he on the Goddard list?' he raised his eyebrows. 'Gives us a bit more to talk to him about, doesn't it?'

'Well,' Morrissey said, 'now isn't that interesting? I wonder if that's how he got involved with our *femme fatale*.' He thought about it. Had the simple selling of a piece of property led to seduction? And if so, what other demands might Marion Walsh have made? The business of selling houses suddenly seemed a more hazardously interesting occupation than he had imagined until now. Unless Cotton and Marion Walsh had known each other before she moved to Little Henge, that was a possibility too.

Brooding, he cracked his fingers; Barrett winced and said, 'Sexy lady buys house and seduces estate agent. Just the thing to bring the tabloids out in a rash. I wonder how she met the other two? If it wasn't the wrong kind of district...' He looked thoughtful. 'Remember last year; the call-girl in Chelwood?'

Morrissey remembered it well. It wasn't every day a local MP resigned, especially one who had always been thought of as squeaky clean. He said severely,

'There's no such thing as the wrong district, not if that's what she's up to.'

'Be a bit of a shock for some of the ladies' committees,' Barrett said casually. 'All those self-righteous matrons compromised by sitting next to her at some lunch or other.'

'That's what you think about ladies' committees, is it?' Morrissey was deceptively mild. 'I'll remember to tell Margaret when I get home, and no doubt she'll put you straight next time you drop in.' Too late Barrett remembered Mrs Morrissey's unflagging support for Oxfam, the NSPCC, and the local animal shelter. He reddened and tried a rapid revision but Morrissey wasn't listening. Instead he heaved himself from the chair.

'Time to see what Cotton has to say for himself.' He saw Barrett's swift glance out of the window at the steam from the canteen ventilator, and smiled wolfishly as he said, 'We'll see him first and eat later.' When Barrett looked stricken he added sadistically, 'Stop thinking about food; fasting is good for the soul—if you believe in such esoteric things.'

Unfed and thirsty, Barrett silently felt for the car keys. Halfway to the first landing the telephone bell turned him back, and when he caught up with Morrissey again he said, 'It was Records, with the Volvo registration—it belongs to Cotton's wife.'

'Coincidences abound,' the chief inspector said. 'And since it seems we're going to rain on his parade, let's hope he has a good umbrella.'

Hearthstone Properties were housed in a double-fronted shop mid way along North Street. The fabric of the building was Victorian, but at some point the original ground-floor frontage had been ripped out and modernised. Since it had become an estate agent's office, change had overtaken it again and the flat windows had given way to Dickensian bows.

Morrissey saw it as a con; an attempt to encourage trust by appealing to a naïve nostalgia for old values. To him, the interior was the real truth; fluorescent lights and bristling efficiency. Ideal for sellers, not always so good for buyers.

Behind the counter a woman was straightening leaflets; Morrissey showed his warrant card and told her briskly, 'Chief Inspector Morrissey to see Mr Cotton, Mr Martin Cotton.' A couple who didn't look much older than Katie gave him a look of curiosity, and then turned back to leafing through a colour catalogue of houses. The woman went away. When she came back she was regretful.

'I'm sorry, but Mr Cotton is busy all day. Would you like to make an appointment for tomorrow?'

Morrissey scowled. 'Would you tell Mr Cotton I have an appointment with him now. His office or mine, it doesn't matter which.' She went away again. This time when she came back she silently lifted the counter flap.

Cotton's office was half-glassed so he could keep an eye on the outer office, but Venetian blinds were there to give him privacy if he wanted it. Was it courtesy or unease that made him want it now? Morrissey wondered, as he accepted the languid handshake.

Heavy-shouldered, short-necked, hair thickly grey, the estate agent didn't look like a Jack the Lad, but there was no telling. Now he said, 'I don't want to seem unhelpful, Chief Inspector, but if you could make it quick: in this business time equals money.'

'In mine it equals hard work,' Morrissey said dryly. 'You handled the sale of a house in Little Henge about a year ago. The Beeches, Hill Road. I'd like a look at the file.'

Cotton sat behind his desk and took his time. He's walking around it, Morrissey thought. He's wondering if there's anything in it to rock his boat. Then, grudgingly, the man said, 'Why would you be interested in it, Chief Inspector? I remember the house; a nice property, but I'm not sure about the file. There is such a thing as confidentiality.'

'There certainly is,' Morrissey agreed gravely. 'And whatever I find in the file will remain confidential—unless it has a bearing on current investigations. Now would you like to produce it for me? Be a bit silly having to get a warrant and waste more valuable time. Yours and mine.'

The estate agent wasn't pleased. 'That assumes it can be found of course. Our old records are kept in the cellar. One of the girls would have to search for it.'

'I can wait,' Morrissey said. 'And I'm sure if Detective Sergeant Barrett helps her look, it will turn up fairly quickly.' Surly-faced, Cotton went out. The girl he sent downstairs was pretty, the chief inspector saw, and he wondered if Barrett would charm anything useful from her.

The estate agent came back, annoyed. 'I'll speak plainly, Chief Inspector. Quite frankly I object to your barging into the office like this and demanding my files. I think I've a right to know what it is you're after.'

'Information, Mr Cotton, that's what policemen are always after. Specifically, information about Mrs Marion Walsh, her friends, and her enemies.' Morrissey studied Cotton carefully. There was already the beginning of darkening on the short neck; put that together with the belligerent stance and you had a man on a short fuse. He prodded. 'Take yourself, for example; I understand you're a very—shall we say close friend of hers?'

'What bloody business is it of yours?'

As if he hadn't heard, Morrissey went on. 'You're a married man, Mr Cotton. How does your wife feel about that friendship? Or is she perhaps ignorant of it?' He stalked carefully. 'Let's take your visits to Little Henge for example; an attractive woman like Marion Walsh would give any wife cause to worry if she knew about them.'

'That must come very close to slander, Chief Inspector.' Cotton flopped back into his chair. 'I'm sure there are rules about that sort of thing.'

'I'm simply asking you to confirm what Mrs Walsh has already told me.' Not strictly true but near enough, Morrissey decided, and watched the dark colour spread.

'I don't believe that, there's nothing to confirm.'

'Then I must tell you that, yesterday morning, an attempt was made on Mrs Walsh's life,' the chief inspector said formally. 'And as a result of that attempt, Mrs Betty Hartley, a daily help, died. You are being questioned, Mr Cotton, as part of a murder inquiry. Now do you understand why I want to know about your friendship with Mrs Walsh?'

Cotton had the appearance of a man on the brink of the abyss, Morrissey thought, and gave him a gentle push. 'A frightened woman isn't usually discreet. Do you still deny there is any relationship between you?'

'There doesn't seem much point, does there? For God's sake sit down, Chief Inspector, and be righteous at a decent level.'

The two chairs before the desk were low-slung tweed and chrome of a type that Morrissey knew would be uncomfortable, but he lowered himself onto one of them and stuck out his long legs. He said, 'One thing that interests me is why, out of all the towns and villages in England, Mrs Walsh chose to live in Little Henge.' He stared at Cotton. 'The pin in a map technique, or would you say she already knew someone?'

'Either, for God's sake; I don't know. I met her when we sold The Beeches.' He half-raised his hands and let them fall. 'She was attractive, and not reticent. One discreet meeting led to another; that sort of thing. I had no idea . . .' his voice trailed off.

No idea of what? thought Morrissey. That Marion Walsh knew all about men; that her income depended on their weaknesses? He said, 'I'll guess, shall I? An invitation to her home, an enjoyable meal, some potent wine—at the time you didn't think too much—but next morning you woke in her bed.'

If that was the way it had happened it was an old story, and proved Marion was no stranger to the game. The chief inspector waited, quietly watching Cotton's struggle inside himself. He wasn't a man who would like to admit to being tricked. Finally Cotton gave a barking laugh. 'Was there a fly on the wall or a spy in the wardrobe?'

Morrissey shook his head. 'Believe me, it's a common story. What happened next?'

'She suggested I should introduce her around. It seemed an innocent request at the time.'

'But not so, with hindsight. When did you start giving her money?'

'I think that's perhaps as far as I want to go.' Cotton shifted in his chair. Morrissey picked up the body language and pressed on.

'Were there small, regular amounts or larger sums she could claim were presents from a good friend?'

'I'm sorry, Chief Inspector; that's enough.'

'And of course there would have to be a hook to dangle you from; photographs perhaps, from that first night?'

Cotton put his hands flat on the desk and said, 'I'm not going to say anything else, Chief Inspector. I have no complaint to make against Mrs Walsh, and I'm not confirming anything you've said.' He pushed himself upright.

Morrissey stood too, glad to separate himself from the chair. 'I don't think there are many gaps left to fill,' he said. The florid face before him now had a tinge of grey and Cotton still hadn't been told about the car.

From the corner of his eye the chief inspector saw Barrett crossing the main office. There was a folder in his hand and he looked satisfied. Morrissey turned to Cotton again. He felt sorry for him now. Sombrely he said, 'A blue Volvo saloon, registration number F413 DWR, was seen parked in Vicarage Lane yesterday morning; it left a little after ten. The driver was in so much of a hurry she scraped the rear bumper of a resident's car. The Volvo is registered to your wife, Mr Cotton. Why would she have been in Little Henge yesterday morning?'

Cotton's voice had lost strength. 'She has a lot of committees, visits a lot of people. I'm sure one of them must involve Little Henge. That has to be the explanation, Chief Inspector. She doesn't know about Marion, I'm certain of it.'

'She will have to be questioned,' Morrissey said. 'I'm sorry.'

'But if you tell her the reason, it could wreck my marriage.'

That was something Cotton should have considered earlier, and something Morrissey couldn't take into account.

'I'll be as circumspect as I can,' he said. 'That's all I can promise. I'll let you have the file back tomorrow.'

'I feel sorry for him,' Barrett said as they drove away. 'I bet he can see his life shredding itself.'

'Let it be a lesson then. Don't get mixed up with promiscuous women, or you might get more than you bargained for.' It was advice to add to Barrett's already guilty overload. Morrissey squinted at him. 'Pretty girl at Hearthstone; did you keep your mind on your work?'

Slowing down Barrett reached into his inside pocket and took out a folded wad of papers. 'Keeps his bank statements down there too,' he said. 'I thought they might be useful.' Morrissey beamed approval. 'Nice one, Neil. Pull into the Boar's Head and I'll buy you a ploughman's.' He added, casually, 'Be seeing her again, will you?'

Coming to a stop between a dilapidated red mini and a new silver Toyota, Barrett gave his chief an innocent smile. 'I might,' he said. 'All in the line of duty of course.'

'Of course,' said Morrissey. 'Anything else would ruin your eyesight.'

ELEVEN

MORRISSEY WONDERED if he had made a mistake; perhaps he should have insisted Cotton returned to his home with them there and then; not to be with his wife but to make certain he couldn't warn her what to expect and then cook up some story. He sighed and shifted in his seat. Something not to mention to Barrett: senior officers were supposed to think of things before, not after it was too late.

But Marjorie Cotton wasn't at home when they got there, and the Volvo wasn't in the garage. Gloomily, Morrissey wandered round the outside of the long, rambling, L-shaped bungalow. Cotton obviously supported a lifestyle that, although not up to the standard of American soaps, must impress Malminster society. The swimming pool itself, under a glass dome, would cost a fortune to heat.

All from selling houses?

'Nice.' Barrett didn't try to keep envy out of his voice.

'Very, but where are the people who look after the place? Don't tell me Mrs Cotton takes care of this little lot on her own.'

'Day off. Shopping. The house-keeper's in bed with the gardener.' Barrett was rarely flippant, but something about the blazoned air of wealth made him so. Somewhere inside the house the telephone began to ring.

Morrissey waited, and the strident sound went on and on and finally stopped. He shook his head at Barrett. 'You've got a rabbit's imagination,' he said. 'Too fertile by far.'

'I don't think so,' said Barrett, beginning to move away. 'We've got an intruder.' He had been looking past Morrissey's shoulder, facing the angle of the house and far enough out to see someone cutting across to a side gate, but he himself was hidden from view by a creepered, ornamental screen. Since late February there had been a spate of daylight break-ins, and the dark blue holdall looked heavy in the man's hand.

It was a thought that communicated itself to Morrissey, and he too began to run across the shaved lawn.

MARION WAS JUMPY without knowing why and the ash-tray was almost full of stubbed-out cigarettes, some only half smoked, others down to the brown filter. Morrissey, she was certain, was trying to panic her. She stared at herself in the mirror, her hair newly styled, carelessly artful. There was no grey, but that was because of the hairdresser's talent—without that those early signs of ageing would be all too apparent and Marion was well aware of it. She had a nest-egg now, the house, a comfortable bank balance. Why go on?

She shuddered, a long, racking movement that seemed to contort each muscle in turn. Give it up now! Get rid of the obscenities that she had learned so painfully to use for her advantage. It hadn't always been so. When memory of her early life forced itself through, like now, she found it hard to believe she had survived it. That she had become the user instead of the used. She supposed that was why she could find no pity for the women.

Rich meal tickets. Lives cushioned until she came along. Who was it said no one truly experienced life except through adversity? And she provided it; that being so, they owed her gratitude not enmity.

She flicked the fat-bellied onyx lighter again and took a deep lungful of smoke from a new cigarette. If the damned policeman were right she wouldn't die from lung cancer at least. Again a shiver and she turned up the heating. If she believed in premonitions...

The chief inspector made Helen Goddard appear innocent as a nun. *Who then?* Poison was a woman's weapon. And why did she feel so damned cold?

The coolness of colours that Marion had once found soothing was now unaccountably hostile. She needed company, but there was no one she could ask to come round.

Perhaps a drink instead? She was lifting it when the doorbell rang and her hand jerked, splashing drops onto her pale dress. She slapped at them with her fingers. There was no need to answer the door; whoever it was would eventually grow tired and go away. She tossed the whisky to the back of her mouth and swallowed, grimacing, then tilted the bottle again.

That bloody bell! Perhaps it was the chief inspector back again—or the sergeant, what was his name? Something to do with houses and little green trees— Garrett—no, *Barrett*. Safe houses. Unaccountably the thought amused her and she drank again. She felt warmer and her fingers were no longer shaking. That was all she had needed—a drink.

And if it were Morrissey at the door...?

Perhaps he had come to offer police protection. She looked at the bottle of Johnnie Walker and saw it was two-thirds empty. Kill the dead soldier, she thought, and watched the rich amber flow once more into her glass. Police protection. Marion remembered the way the chief inspector's clothes seemed shrunk on him, all arms and legs and awkward angles. A big man. Made raunchy as always by the whisky, she thought about bed. Bed and Morrissey. And it was that thought that took her into the kitchen.

She recognised the outlined silhouette beyond the frosted glass and felt disappointment. Ungraciously she snatched open the door, and said acidly, 'Oh, it's you. You'd better come in.'

MORRISSEY HAD KILLED two birds with one stone and was quietly satisfied. Inside the bungalow one Ray-

mond Miller was cuffed and waited to be collected.
Barrett watched over him. The blue holdall was
empty, its contents laid out on the kitchen table. Some
Georgian silver, a collection of jade netsuke, three
Meissen figurines—all of them of considerable worth,
but there was more. Miller hadn't been choosy about
items of jewellery, he had just taken the leather case
and all it held. Morrissey's eyebrows had risen. Some
of the pieces, unless they were paste which he
doubted, had deserved to be kept in a safe and not on
a dressing table. Or had Mrs Cotton left in an uncar-
ing hurry?

There were photographs in heavy silver frames too;
in one of them, a wedding photograph, Morrissey
recognised Cotton. And Cotton, who seemed to be
having a very bad day, was on his way from the office. So was Inspector Beckett who would be very
happy to see Miller and wrap up his case.

In the meantime the chief inspector was not a man
to let opportunity slip by, and he was quietly and at
speed going through the ransacked house.

The photograph he found in the medium-sized envelope had a five-day-old postmark, and showed
Martin Cotton had a degree of sexual athleticism not
readily apparent from his everyday image. It also
showed Marion Walsh, and on the back her address
had been written in uneven capitals.

He no longer had to ask if Mrs Cotton knew.

And when he showed it to the estate agent, what would his reaction be? Mixed in with the censoriousness Morrissey felt was a flick of pity.

Mrs Cotton's Volvo had been seen in Little Henge, and here was evidence that gave her a motive to hate.

And now she had left her home insecure and gone where?

Sighing heavily, he used the bedroom extension to telephone Blake and ask for a constable to be sent to the Walsh house. Then he went back to Barrett and his prisoner and settled down to wait.

First came Beckett and DC Smythe, and almost immediately afterwards, Cotton, filling the kitchen. Cotton looked haggard.

'Where's Marjorie?' was the first thing he asked. Morrissey shook his head.

'Your wife isn't here, and neither is her car. I hoped you'd know where she might be.'

Beckett said, 'There seems to have been easy access into the bungalow, sir, and the alarm system wasn't triggered. Could you check if it had been turned on?'

Cotton shook his head. 'She must have forgotten. The system is set up to automatically trigger a telephone alarm at the office during the daytime, as well as making a hell of a noise here.'

'You have a safe, I suppose; would your wife's jewellery normally be there?'

Cotton's eyes swept the table and saw the leather case. 'Yes,' he said. 'I suppose I'd better check.'

'I didn't find no safe,' Miller said surlily. 'Stupid cow had it in the bedroom. She off her trolley wheels or somethink?' His eyes on the estate agent were insolent, mocking and accusing at the same time. Cotton whitened but didn't trouble to answer, simply walking out of the room with Beckett.

'How come I got all the top brass out then?' Miller shifted on the wooden chair. 'Somethink else going on? There is, isn't there? Might know somethink, mightn't I? Might be worth a bit of time.'

'Might be worth another six months if you don't shut up,' said Barrett.

Morrissey's eyes were half closed, impatient and trying to contain it, wanting to get Miller out of the way. DC Smythe said, 'What might you know?'

'Nothink. Trying it on for size, aren't I?'

Cotton came back having seen the mess in the other rooms, the upturned drawers and overturned mattresses, annoyed that when Beckett and Smythe took Miller away there would still be Morrissey, patiently waiting. He began to examine the items on the table, nodding as he handled them. 'Yes,' he said finally, 'it's all from here.'

'We have to take it with us. I'm sorry, but it's classed as evidence,' Beckett said and looked at Smythe. 'Got the list and receipt?' Silently the DC handed over the triplicate form, and Morrissey sighed. Five minutes would see them gone.

Five minutes and Cotton would know just how bloody stupid he'd been.

'Should the house have been empty?' he asked Cotton. 'No gardener, no daily?'

'The daily comes in the mornings, and it isn't the gardener's day. I don't understand why the alarm wasn't on. Marjorie is usually the one who double-checks everything.'

'Upset perhaps, and in a hurry,' Morrissey suggested passively, biding his time, seeing Cotton wince as metal scraped on metal in the holdall.

''Appen your missus has gone to see the fancy bit,' Miller sniped as Smythe hauled him upright. 'Could have done a nice bit of black there if I'd took that picture. Ought to thank me for minding me own business.'

Beckett shot a glance at Morrissey and got an almost imperceptible shake of the head. 'Come on,' he said, 'out,' and gave Miller a shove.

'What picture? Wait!' Cotton said. 'I want to know what he's talking about.'

Miller was hustled out of the door, and as Beckett followed he told Cotton, 'The chief inspector can tell you what you want to know,' and snapped it closed behind him.

Morrissey said, 'I found a photograph, Mr Cotton, sent by post to your wife a few days ago. I have it here if you'd like to see it.' Carefully he laid the black and white enlargement on the kitchen table, face up. Barrett twisted his head to see. There was speculation in his eyes when he lifted them to Cotton.

The estate agent's cheeks seemed to shrink. 'I—I...'
He grabbed the photograph and would have ripped it
if Morrissey hadn't snatched it back.

'No, sir; I'm sorry, but this is evidence too. Evidence that your wife knew about Mrs Walsh before
the attempt on her life.'

'You're mad,' Cotton said shakily. 'Marjorie
wouldn't... Couldn't... Where would she get hold
of... what was it? What kind of poison?'

'You tell me, sir. I don't remember having said it
was poison.'

'I...I...' The veins in the short neck were becoming prominent as dusky patches discoloured the
estate agent's face. Barrett pulled out a chair and
Cotton flopped onto it. Morrissey took a mug from
the draining rack and filled it with water from the tap;
Cotton waved it away but then took it and drank
quickly.

'If you'd like to set the alarm system, sir, I'd like
you to come back to the station with me and let me
have a full account of your movements yesterday.'

'I don't see...'

'If you wouldn't mind, sir.' Morrissey had an implacability of face and voice that made the light of
battle die from Cotton's eyes.

'I'll just be a minute,' he said stiffly and went out
into the central hall.

Barrett looked at the chief inspector. 'Mrs Walsh
could have told him.'

'Very probably, but he's frightened, and a frightened man is likely to give out more information than one who isn't, and I think Mr Cotton can tell us quite a bit more than he has already. I just wish he was a healthier colour.'

'He can't be that unfit, sir,' Barrett turned the photograph so that it faced him. 'Not if he can manage that.'

Morrissey sighed. 'Cause and effect, Neil,' he said gravely. 'Cause and effect.'

TWELVE

IT FELL TO Barrett to take Martin Cotton to an interview room, to see the man's eyes freeze in fascination on the tape recorder when he started it going. The glaze of sweat on his face had grown heavier, and the sergeant had felt it politic to provide the mug of hot, sweet tea that stood almost untouched beside Cotton. He could no longer doubt that the estate agent was a funny colour.

Police Constable Pace was doing desk duty, filling in for a DC who had found himself pushed through a plate glass window. Next week he would be on nights again and he wasn't looking forward to it. It hadn't been too bad before he was married, but now... Well, now it was different, and Ruth... He pushed that thought away, he didn't want to think about what his pretty red-haired wife might do, left to her own devices. It was disloyal, it was chauvinist, it wasn't what marriage was all about, and thinking of it tore a hole in the bottom of his stomach.

Sexual freedom had seemed a very modern and wholly desirable agreement to make before they were married, but things had changed—on his part at least. Ruth had said it was a primitive reversal to territorial rights; a denial of female equality. Sometimes Pace wished she wasn't so well educated.

Morrissey had been given part of the message from Little Henge while he was still in the car with Barrett and Cotton, but at that point, unwilling for the estate agent to hear more, he had snapped, 'Hold it for now, I'll be at the station in two minutes and I'll take it then.'

Barrett had accepted that as a signal to turn on the siren and put his foot down.

Now the chief inspector was looking for a driver while Barrett dealt with Cotton, and Pace was the first man he saw. It was a coincidence that pleased him; he held the opinion that the young constable's potential hadn't been fully noticed, and with an opening for a CID Aide on the cards Morrissey would have a chance to see what he was made of.

'Fast but safe,' he said as they got into the car. 'Into Little Henge, turn right at the Community Centre, and pull up at the house next to the vicarage.'

Pace nodded and drove smoothly out of the yard, turning on the blue flashing light. 'New development, sir?' he asked.

'Yes,' Morrissey said grimly, uncomfortably aware that by the nature of things brick-bats would start coming his way. He had anticipated this might happen, but given the circumstances didn't think he could have prevented it. Then he amended his thoughts. He had anticipated the event—not the way of it—and Marion Walsh had refused his advice.

There was a uniformed constable at the gate, and another, palely perspiring, outside the kitchen door of the Walsh house. Morrissey, as he went inside, said with gruff understanding, 'Get down to the pod and get a pot of tea inside you. Say it's my orders. And wipe the sweat off your face.'

'Thank you, sir.' The hand that fumbled for and found the handkerchief was unsteady, Morrissey saw that too as he turned away. To Pace, following behind, he said, 'Strong stomach?'

'Sir?'

'If not, you'd better wait here.'

'I'll be fine, sir.' They were words he regretted, and yet, as Morrissey approvingly noted, after the first upheaval of bile, swiftly swallowed, he kept control.

Inspector Blake was standing at the nearest of the two sitting-room windows, looking out across the garden. The window was open and a coolly fresh breeze washed in, but did nothing to disperse the sickly sweet smell that hung on the air.

He had done as Morrissey had asked and sent a constable to the Walsh house, and when the man had radioed in, retching as he spoke, Blake had got there as fast as he could. He hadn't expected the sheer brutality of what he found. And when he had made quite certain there was no one else in the house, and Morrissey and the scene of crime team were on their way, he had opened the sitting-room window and stood stolidly with his back to the thing on the floor, and asked himself why the hell he wanted to be a policeman.

Now he turned and saw the flat control on Morrissey's face, and asked himself how many more years it would be before he could face this situation with the same command.

'Thanks, Alan,' Morrissey said. 'Anything I need to know?'

Blake shook his head. 'Nothing has been touched. I had a look around the place; empty of course, but the main bedroom has been turned over. Pretty thoroughly too.'

'No one seen coming or going?'

'I'll have to get back to you on that, but I'd say no so far. WPC Yarby has been checking round and she hasn't radioed in yet. I told her to ask about the Volvo at the same time.'

'Give me a buzz if there is anything,' Morrissey said as more feet came through the kitchen. He was suddenly glad not to be a photographer. Blake nodded as the room filled with men and the minutiae of a murder hunt began again, painstaking, thorough, every detail charted, photographed, examined.

It was Pace's first opportunity to see what he had learned from textbooks put into action, and his eyes missed nothing. That was something else the chief inspector approved of as he left the busyness of the sitting-room and went upstairs alone.

As Blake had said, the main bedroom revealed
chaos. Every drawer had been emptied, every cupboard. The mattress had been tipped from the bed,
the carpet lifted. The safe had been under the carpet,
let into the floorboards, about a foot square in size
and it was wide open. There were still papers inside,
packets that had been looked at and tossed back, vel-
vet jewellery boxes, their contents untouched. Whoever had done this had wanted something specific;
hadn't been interested in money. Had wanted something that would have incriminated either themselves
or someone close to them.

Could a woman be responsible for the horror
downstairs? A woman made frantic enough to jab a
broken whisky bottle again and again into the face
and neck of Marion Walsh?

Or a man destroying the thing he feared?

Through the window the Goddard house looked
down at him, its windows blind and empty. What of
Helen? he wondered. Had she decided yet whether to
stay or go?

He told himself it was no concern of his, except in
as much as he needed to know where she and her
husband could be found.

The other bedrooms appeared to be untouched,
and the bathroom too had no sign of disturbance. He
peered into the shower and found it dry. Whoever
killed Marion Walsh must have been soaked in blood;
it had splashed everywhere in the room downstairs,

the walls, the furniture, congealed on the carpet. An abattoir, he thought, and the same smell.

Could anyone in that state have walked out of the house, got into a car and driven away without being seen?

Perhaps—if the car had been parked in the lane by the side gate.

He went back downstairs and asked that the bedroom too be dusted for prints, and its contents photographed. He was doing that when the police surgeon arrived, saw the body, and swore with a quiet and contained fluency that Morrissey hadn't known he possessed.

'Jim?'

Reed turned his head and looked at the chief inspector. 'I'm beginning to think of early retirement,' he said. 'I'm getting too old for this sort of thing.'

'You're younger than I am,' Morrissey came to his side.

'I've always been too old.' Reed squatted carefully; there were shards of broken whisky bottle embedded in the carpet, scattered under the small table. Morrissey forced himself to Reed's level. He hadn't wanted this close a view of the dead woman's injuries but he felt an odd compulsion to share his friend's repugnant chore.

This time Pace didn't look.

With hands protected by rubber gloves the police doctor delicately moved the mutilated head, and Morrissey saw another injury, a flattening at the left side above her ear, a discoloured splinter that looked like bone.

'Be glad,' Reed said. 'It looks as if the first injury was a crushing blow, probably with the intact bottle. The force fractured the skull in the temporal region. She would have been unconscious when the other injuries were inflicted.'

'Could a woman use that force?'

'Given the right build, or the right degree of anger. It looks as if the mutilations were done in a frenzy. If they weren't, you're looking for a very cool psychopath. Whoever it was would have needed to be roughly the same height, possibly taller, to get that angle on the bottle. The injury extends downwards from the temple behind the left ear. And right handed.'

'Not from behind and upward?'

Reed frowned thoughtfully at the chief inspector. 'Trust you to complicate things. The post-mortem will decide one way or the other. That's the best I can do.'

'Time?'

'Not long. Less than two hours.'

This morning Marion had said she was going to the hairdressers. Morrissey suspected that afterwards she had probably spoken to Martin Cotton; possibly warned Turner and Moxon too. And then she had come home and all unsuspecting opened the door to someone she knew.

Poison first, then this. Was he looking for one murderer or two?

Reed got to his feet and Morrissey rose with him. 'At least I've finished now,' the doctor said, stripping off his gloves with care. 'You're just starting.' He shoved the gloves into a plastic bag and stuffed it into a side pocket in his case. 'It's quite a step from cyanide to that kind of violence,' he said, 'but given the right incentive...'

Morrissey nodded. 'What I need is a crystal ball.'

'I'll see you later,' Reed said. 'Try not to find me more work I can do without. If I hadn't had a stint in pathology you'd have had to get the Home Office wallah for this lot.'

The Home Office laboratories and the region's forensic pathologists were based at Wetherby and, until he quit six years ago, Reed had been one of them. Now he had turned to healing people instead and felt himself a happier man.

The chief inspector said, 'Lets you keep your hand in,' and Reed shook his head.

'I can do without it,' he promised, and Morrissey stood at the open door, glad to get the smell of the room out of his nostrils, and watched the doctor drive away.

When the ransacked bedroom had been dusted and puffed for fingerprints, and its disorder photographed, Morrissey felt he could move around freely and have a good look at what was left in the safe.

The packets held photographs similar to that sent to Marjorie Cotton. Morrissey suspected they were there to ensure that if the voluntary 'presents' had stopped, Marion had the means to restart them. There were letters dealing with the house purchase, bank statements, a wedding certificate. The jewellery alone would be worth several thousand pounds, Morrissey guessed, and he wondered who would inherit. Then the thought came that Betty Hartley's son hadn't turned up yet. He was thinking about that when Barrett telephoned and told him Cotton had had a coronary in the interview room.

'The doctors are wanting to know about his wife,' Barrett said. 'From what they say it's a bit touch and go.'

'Tell them we'll find her as soon as we can,' said Morrissey wearily, 'then get someone to relieve you and get over here. It's going to be a long day.'

THIRTEEN

IT WOULD ALL have to be done again. All the men sent back out, house-to-house, same questions, different time and place. Morrissey could imagine the groans that would cause; no one liked to knock on doors. He watched the zipped-up body bag carried out of the house and meditated on the thought that two days ago he had wondered who would mourn Betty, and now the same question had risen in his mind about Marion Walsh. A knot of people were gathered near the gate watching, their faces question marks of curiosity, and there were others across the road, paused on their way to or from the few shops.

Two deaths in as many days—there was fodder for gossip for a long time to come.

Morrissey was picking up intangible undercurrents again. It was in the faces of the people at the gate, and in the way they stood. The mood outside Betty Hartley's cottage had been one of excitement almost, but now it was something else. Uneasiness?

It would be too imaginative to say that in some strange way the village had changed its being; put on another face. But Little Henge had been forced to contain horror, and because of it there was an unrest in the air, a sick fever that hadn't yet reached crisis.

When would it? When would it break and let healing begin? He shook himself mentally. Introspection wasn't part of police work, painstaking piecing together was.

When Barrett arrived the sightseers were gone, moved on efficiently. His nose twitched when he stepped into the house; there was a strong, sweet smell that he recognised unwillingly: that of a butcher's shop on a hot day.

He saw the carefully drawn outline where Marion had lain, the ugliness of the broken bottle, and the dark stains, and then he remembered Marion Walsh as she had looked that first day; provocative, very sure of herself.

The SOCOs were almost finished, the photographer packing away his equipment. David Pace was watching, his back to the door. Barrett recognised him and turned away to look for Morrissey. He found him in the main bedroom, carefully putting packets, papers, and miscellaneous jewellery cases into a Tesco carrier bag.

The chief inspector looked up when Barrett came in. He asked, 'Did you send someone over to Cotton's to wait for the wife?'

'A mobile with a WPC.' Barrett stared round the bedroom. 'This is a mess.'

'Isn't it though; be nice to know what he was looking for. Probably photographs. His. There's a camera set up in the wardrobe.'

Barrett raised his eyebrows and went across to the wide unit. When the room was in good order the mirrored doors would reflect the bed and everything that happened on it.

'Middle door,' Morrissey instructed. 'You'll find the mirror is observation glass.'

Barrett opened it and saw the built-in camera.

'Not a beginner, was she?' he said.

'Be nice to know who set it up for her.'

'Goddard,' Barrett suggested. 'He's the obvious one. Where did she get the glass though?'

'Any good glass merchant,' the chief inspector said dourly. 'Somewhere around ten pounds a foot.' He watched Barrett fiddle with the camera and said irritably, 'It's on an automatic timer, one exposure every thirty seconds. Isn't technology wonderful?'

Barrett's surprise showed, and Morrissey chose not to disillusion him by admitting he'd been primed by the forensic photographer. He said, 'I'm leaving the rest of the house search to you and Pace. You know what to look for, addresses, letters, photographs, anything that might be helpful. When you've finished make sure everything's secure. I'm going back to Malminster to see Turner and Moxon.'

'Yes, sir.' Crisp acknowledgement. Then, 'Why Pace? He isn't CID.'

Morrissey squinted at him. 'Difficulties between you, are there?'

Barrett looked uncomfortable. 'No. I just thought...'

'He has the making of a good policeman. I'll be advising him to apply for CID Aide when it comes up next month.'

'It's usually a bit of a scramble.'

'Easier if a senior officer puts in a good word,' said Morrissey. 'He's not been married long, I hear. Pretty, is she, his wife? I expect you've seen her.'

'Oh, I, er... Once... A couple of times when she's called in at the station.'

'And pretty?'

'I suppose so. It's um ... It's not ...'

'No it isn't, is it?' said Morrissey. 'But then that's something we both know, isn't it?'

As Barrett exercised his right to remain silent, Morrissey allowed himself a certain grim satisfaction. Put two and two together and sometimes five is the right answer, as it had been this time. Sheer co-incidence of course, but Barrett didn't know that. When this was over...

'When all this is wrapped up we'll have a talk,' the chief inspector said decisively. 'We'll have a good look at career prospects from the very basic angle of birds and bees. In the meantime, help Pace along, will you? And when you've both finished you can come back to the station in your car—I'll be driving the other back myself.'

'Yes, sir.' Barrett watched Morrissey's retreating back. Omniscient. He'd heard others say that about the chief inspector, now he had it proved. If Eve, he thought, had taken the apple and stuffed it down the bloody serpent's throat, it would have saved a lot of trouble.

Morrissey's thoughts were much different on the drive back to Malminster, and concentrated entirely on trying to make some kind of order out of seeming chaos. He handed in the jewellery from the Walsh house and saw it into the police safe, neatly docketed and signed in before he took the photographs and other papers to his office.

He reflected that earlier that day he had intended asking the Met to check on Marion's old London address. Now he had more to ask of them and a greater urgency. Thank God for modern communication systems which speeded up the passing of long and complicated information. And thank God too he didn't have to operate them.

Before locking the photographs in his desk he took out two, one of Turner, one of Moxon. Proof positive, should either attempt to deny those things he was sure they would rather forget.

But Turner, who owned the ritziest jewellery shop in Malminster, was in Salzburg and so was his wife, and had been away for a week. Morrissey stood in the hall of the detached Victorian villa and waited for the housekeeper to find the name of their hotel, and while he waited he eyed the pile of mail on the hall table. One envelope, brown and rigid, was addressed to Emily Turner in the same almost illegible scrawl as that sent to Marjorie Cotton.

Quietly he took it from the pile. Turner might be a fool but his wife didn't deserve to pay for it.

When the housekeeper returned he was smoothing his hair in the mirror, vaguely surprised by the amount of shirt cuff that showed between wrist and jacket sleeve.

Bernard Moxon lived in a new executive development on the eastern outskirts of Malminster. A tightly small grouping where it was expected only the 'right' people would live by virtue of financial exclusion. Unfortunately the land behind the development belonged to the local council, and Morrissey had heard plans were already afoot to build an overflow council estate on the site. When that news leaked out there would be quite a furore.

Moxon's house was double-fronted in rustic brick, its woodwork fashionable mahogany. The brass bell-push shone mirror bright and Morrissey caught himself dusting off his finger before he touched it.

When the door opened, a middle-aged woman in tweeds fixed a baleful eye on Morrissey and said, 'It's about time: you were supposed to be here an hour ago.'

The chief inspector offered a courteous denial and showed his warrant card. 'I'd like to see Mr Bernard Moxon if he's at home.'

She compressed her lips and for a minute looked as if she would close the door, but then thought better of it.

'My brother has problems enough without them being added to,' she said. 'Unless it's very important...'

'And also very private,' he said firmly, and with his hand on the door stepped into the hall and looked around. The house, despite its up-market price, was nothing like as spacious as his own. If he stretched out his arms he would be able to touch both sides of the hall. For some reason the knowledge gave him a perverse satisfaction.

'Would you tell your brother I'm here?'

Disgruntled she snapped the door closed and stalked past him, opening another on the right. Now her voice was almost cooing. 'Bernie, dear, there's a policeman here. Shall I send him away?'

From behind her Morrissey pushed the door open further. He said, 'Good evening, Mr Moxon, I know you won't mind sparing me a little time.'

Moxon was a speculator, a property dealer. Once or twice he had skated on thin ice, so far without falling through. But one thing was certain, he wouldn't like being blackmailed. Now he had a cut-glass tumbler half full of amber liquid in his hand. Hunched in the leather chair he looked rather like a malevolent turtle, his hooded eyes full of dislike.

'It would appear I have no choice in the matter.' The eyes moved away. 'Thank you, Joyce, I'd rather we were alone.'

This time there was no demur and she closed the door soundlessly.

'Sit down,' Moxon told the chief inspector.

Morrissey lowered himself onto a high-backed chair and sat there still and solid as a jailer, eyes watchful, and said, 'I believe that for almost a year you have been acquainted with Mrs Marion Walsh, of The Beeches, Little Henge.'

'Acquainted.' Moxon lifted the glass towards Morrissey and then took a drink, narrow face expressionless. 'What a beautifully ambivalent word that is. Expand it a little.'

'More than acquainted. Shall we say intimately connected?'

Moxon's hands, as he raised them, were almost hairless, long fingered and well manicured. 'You may if you wish, Chief Inspector. I don't believe I have any need to say anything.'

Morrissey sighed. He had hoped that Moxon wouldn't make things harder than they needed to be. How much perversity was natural to the man's character and how much came from a bottle?

He tried another approach. 'I am sure you are just as aware as I am, sir, of the rules governing police investigations.'

A nod.

'That being so...'

'That being so, mind your own bloody business. No offence.'

'It is my business. You were introduced to Mrs Walsh by another acquaintance, Mr Martin Cotton.'

'I've met any number of people through Martin. I don't remember them all.'

'But you remember Mrs Walsh. Where is Mrs Moxon?' Morrissey said softly. 'Is she at home?'

Moxon's skin darkened. 'That's certainly none of your business, but as it happens she's away for a few days visiting family.'

The chief inspector raised an interrogative eyebrow. 'A decision she made after an envelope was sent to her containing a photograph?'

'My brother-in-law...'

'Is the chief constable. Yes, sir, I know. I have another photograph here you might find interesting.' He held it between his middle finger and thumb. Moxon's eyes rounded and he snatched at it, but Morrissey drew his hand back and waited. For a second it looked as though the other man would lever himself out of his chair, but then his anger abated and he sank back.

'How many of the damned things are there?' he breathed, and topped up his glass. 'If it's somebody's idea of blackmail, it's a clumsy attempt.'

'Were you aware that Mrs Walsh had photographs?'

'Yes.'

'You did nothing about it?'

'She had nothing to gain by using them.'

'Except as a threat.'

'Except as a threat. Dead geese don't lay eggs.'

'And of course you paid well for Mrs Walsh's services?'

'That is a private matter between myself and Mrs Walsh,' Moxon snapped, 'and no concern at all of the police.'

'But I'm afraid it is, Mr Moxon. Marion Walsh was murdered earlier today.'

Moxon was drinking and the liquid slopped down his chin, and stained the light maroon tie. 'How? How was she murdered?'

'Several blows to the head,' said Morrissey.

'Burglary!' Moxon said feverishly. 'It has to be. I warned her to make the place more secure.'

'When did you see her last?'

'A week ago.'

'I'd like to know your movements for today if you don't mind.'

Moxon glared, then the hands flapped again. 'I'm public minded; ask anybody. And I find it insulting to be asked that. As if you think I...'

'I don't think anything, sir. It's standard procedure. I have to ask the same question of everyone who knew Mrs Walsh.'

'I spent the morning at my place of business and came home at one for lunch. I've been here ever since.' He sprang to his feet and wrenched open the door, calling down the passageway. 'Joyce! Joyce! Come and tell the chief inspector I came home at one, and I've been here all day.'

'Of course you have!' said his sister, thrusting out of the kitchen with floured hands. 'You haven't been out at all. Why? Why would anyone ask?'

'Thank you,' said Morrissey over Moxon's shoulder. 'You can go back now.' She hesitated, and went back to her baking.

Moxon turned with a look of sly triumph. 'You see, Chief Inspector. Exactly as I said.'

'Yes sir; *exactly* as you said. Do you still have the photograph that was sent to your wife?'

'I burned it. Why in God's name would I keep it?'

'If you had there might have been fingerprints. I'm sure you'd be happier knowing who sent it, Mr Moxon, but I may need to speak to your wife later. Can you tell me where she is?'

He reddened uncomfortably. 'Why should she be brought into it? There's enough damage done already. I don't even know... Our marriage is a shambles because of this.'

There was indignation in his stance, there was anger, but there wasn't a trace of guilt for the relationship that had caused his wife's distress.

Morrissey squared his chin. 'Her address, Mr Moxon.'

The smaller man's eyes slithered away. 'She's at my brother-in-law's,' he said bitterly. 'Where else?'

FOURTEEN

SOMEWHERE deep down inside, Marjorie Cotton was afraid; but then she had been afraid for a long time, of many and varied things. She had been afraid of the intimacies of marriage, and desperately afraid of childbirth; sometimes she had wondered if it was fear itself that caused her to miscarry three times. And then Charlie had been born and for a long time she lived and moved in a normal world where fear had no part. Until Martin decided she was too clinging, and Charlie too soft, and chose boarding school to teach him aggression.

Now he was sixteen, and his father's clone, just as Martin had wanted.

Then had come the fear that Martin would leave her—although when she was honest with herself she knew that was something she could live with; the real fear was being alone.

She knew Martin had sex with other women. Guilt and gratitude mixed themselves; guilt that he needed to, and gratitude that she escaped the chore.

Then the photograph had come. She recognised Marion without difficulty; a big, brassy blonde whose throaty voice acted like a honey trap for men, and she wasn't the only wife in Malminster to feel that.

Amazingly, for the first time in her life, fear hadn't been the strongest emotion; instead anger had been supreme.

She had driven to Little Henge once before, intent on flinging the photograph in Marion Walsh's face. Who else could have sent it? But instead she had seen Helen Goddard hesitating outside the door and she had lost courage.

Today she had returned and found the kitchen door ajar, and when no one had answered the bell she had gone in. Her loud "hello" brought only silence. Hesitatingly, thinking how foolish the word was in the circumstances, and when there was still only silence, she had gone into the sitting-room.

It had taken a minute before her eyes accepted that something terrible had happened. She saw blood and splintered bone, and the jagged, broken bottle. Handling it had been automatic, as though some invisible gear had slid into place, and she had held it in her hand, fascinated by its sharp teeth.

Some far corner of her mind was surprised by the amount of blood. It had got onto her clothes and hands, and she had wiped her hands down the front of her coat like a child with sticky fingers.

Marjorie had no memory of going back to her car or driving it away. Her first and last conscious act after leaving Little Henge was to pull into a lay-by to be violently sick, and then fear had swamped everything, even the memory of Marion.

When she got back into the car it was on the passenger side. She hoped Daddy wouldn't be long and wondered where he had gone; it wasn't like him to go away and leave her in the car alone. And she felt so ill.

A little after six, almost four hours after she had left the Walsh house, a police car pulled into the lay-by behind her and the two men in it got out and walked slowly to the Volvo. When one of them opened the passenger door she began to cry, and said she was waiting for her Daddy and he'd been gone a very long time.

FIFTEEN

MORRISSEY WENT STRAIGHT to the hospital. It was something of a first, he realised grimly, to have both a husband and a wife hospitalised on the same day. But at least the wheels were moving smoothly now; Mrs Cotton's clothing had already been sent to forensic, and the Volvo towed into the police garage.

There was a WPC by the bed in the hospital room. When the chief inspector went in she was flicking through the pages of a magazine and stood up guiltily, setting the glossy down on the locker. 'I was just...'

'Why not?' he said gruffly. 'Nothing else to do while you wait.'

Relieved, she relaxed. 'She hasn't opened her eyes since I got here; the doctors had already shot her full of something before I arrived.'

Morrissey's mouth turned down. It was no more than he had expected, but he would have liked to have seen the woman's mental state for himself and not relied solely on hearsay. He studied the woman's face. With her eyes closed they looked sunken in their sockets. Someone had washed her face for it was clear of make-up and her skin looked sallow. Forty—forty-five? She moved restlessly and flung out one arm, almost hitting him as he bent over her.

'Let me know if she wakes,' he said, moving away.

The doctor wouldn't commit himself when that would be, but was certain it wouldn't be for the rest of the night, protesting that the amount of mental trauma exhibited had demanded the heaviest sedation.

'That might be,' Morrissey said, 'but I have to find the answers to a particularly brutal murder. I want to talk to Mrs Cotton as soon as she wakes.'

The doctor, professionally indifferent and tired after a long shift, pointed out that Morrissey's wish could be difficult, since his patient had regressed to being a twelve-year-old.

'A temporary thing, surely?' the chief inspector pressed. 'When she wakes up she'll remember what happened.'

'I stopped trying to predict what the human brain would do years ago.' The doctor shrugged. 'I've asked a consultant psychiatrist to see her in the morning; that's the best I can do for you.'

And when Morrissey trod the long corridor to Intensive Care he fared little better. Martin Cotton certainly couldn't be questioned, he was told crisply. Not for at least three days. But he did learn about their son Charlie, and get the name of his boarding school.

Barrett was back at the office before him, sitting elbows on desk with a mug of tea and a thick chip butty. Morrissey's own hunger rose. Chip butties,

oozing cholesterol, were a canteen speciality introduced at roughly the same time as the fat cook from
Bradford.

He eyed Barrett in disgust. The sergeant was bliss-
fully impervious. 'Want me to get you one?'

'Why not?' Morrissey sighed. 'It's better than
having to sit and watch. Pace finished shift?'

'Yep. Six o'clock.' Barrett picked up the phone and
asked for two butties and a coffee. Morrissey didn't
bother asking who the second was for.

'Did you turn up anything at the Walsh house?'

'A wedding photograph, taken outside a Registry
Office by the look of it. Household bills, bank statements. No letters, no diary, no address book. Someone could have been there before us, of course. The
bedroom bothers me.' Barrett stopped chewing and
frowned. 'I mean it had really been turned over, but
not the rest of the house.'

'Yes.'

'But why?'

'You tell me, Neil.' He looked sideways at the PC
who had come in with a tray. 'Thanks.' Then, pushing one plate forward, said to Barrett, 'I suppose this
is yours?'

'Breakfast,' the sergeant said cryptically. 'I don't
think it was wrecked just to find the safe, and a
stranger to the place wouldn't have known to look
there anyway. If I had to guess I'd say it was spite, but
I can't tell you why.' He brought an envelope folder

across to Morrissey's desk. 'It's all in here, everything we found that might be useful.'

Morrissey flicked it open and peered inside. 'What's this doing here?' he said. Barrett shrugged.

'It was at the back of a drawer. It seemed such an unlikely thing for her to have I thought I'd bring it back. I mean I can't see her wearing it herself, can you?'

Morrissey turned the leather ring over between his fingers, recognising it from when he was a scout, and tried to imagine why Marion Walsh had wanted a woggle. Stock in trade perhaps, like the gymslip and the leather thigh boots. He put it down on his desk and said, 'Mrs Cotton has turned up by the way; in a lay-by, very bloody, and apparently out of her mind.'

Barrett was wary. 'But something you know stops her fitting into the picture?' he suggested.

'The bottle wielder, according to Doc Reed, must have been roughly the same height, or taller than Marion Walsh. Mrs Cotton can't be more than five-two, five-three. No. There's something we've missed.' He moved the empty plate and pot to the side of his desk and pulled Cotton's statement towards him. 'Did you get anything useful before he flaked out?'

'Not much. She was into him for a hundred a week. Be interesting to know how much the other two paid for it. Did they own up or plead innocent?'

'Turner's abroad, Moxon owned up. There was nothing else he could do in the circumstances. The point is,' he unlocked the top desk drawer and took out the packets of photographs, 'these were in the safe. Cotton, Turner, Moxon. Why leave them to point a finger?'

'None of Goddard,' Barrett said.

'No. But that was all round the village. No point having the means of blackmail if the cat's out of the bag, and that poses another problem. Mrs Turner and Mrs Moxon got a photograph too. Moxon burned the one his wife was sent, but...' He picked up the brown envelope he had brought in from the car. 'This was at the Turner house, unopened.'

Barrett looked at the print. French maids and bondage; he wondered what Moxon's kink had been.

'We can take it as read Marion didn't send them,' Morrissey said. 'She wouldn't cut off her own money supply.'

Too right, Barrett thought. But they had to be developed and printed, and Goddard had a dark room. He passed the thought on. As far as he was concerned the chief inspector had been far too gentlemanly with the Goddards, and the wife in particular.

But Morrissey wasn't being blind; the thought that Goddard's role might have included photographic processing had hit him as soon as he had found the packets of prints in the open safe. But it still left Goddard a long way from murder.

Morrissey's problem was that Helen Goddard and the strange urge he felt to protect her had clouded his thoughts.

He shook himself mentally. Good detectives weren't made by having their ideas curbed, and, with that thought in mind, he decided to let Barrett have his head, and suggested, 'See Goddard tomorrow and find out what his movements were. And then run a check on both him and the other three; go as far back as you can. Something might shake out.'

'How was Cotton?' Barrett asked, unable to shake off guilt that he had ridden him too hard. Morrissey took things more slowly, and the sergeant knew he would have to learn to curb his own impatience if he wanted promotion. If he'd been gentler . . . The coronary would have happened sooner or later, but maybe not then.

'Not good,' Morrissey said. 'There's a son at boarding school. I shall have to talk to the headmaster; the boy has a right to know, just in case.'

'There's another lab report in,' Barrett said quickly, pushing his thoughts away from Cotton. 'It's a bit—um... Well I don't understand it.' His fingers reached for the Hartley file. 'A higher concentration of cyanide in the char's cup of coffee than in the milk bottle. It doesn't sound right.'

It sounded illogical; another setback that Morrissey could have done without. He re-read the report and glimpsed a possible, bizarre answer. For an instant the darkness he had sensed at Betty Hartley's cottage was back in his mind; something was twisted, and the more he uncovered, the further away he seemed to be from the truth. And he didn't like it.

SIXTEEN

THE WOGGLE WAS on the chest of drawers close to the tray that held his keys and loose change. He had found it the previous night when he emptied his pockets, and felt momentary annoyance that it was there and not with the rest of the things from the Walsh house.

He was carefully gathering up the small coins when Michael came in, wheedling to use some of his father's after-shave.

'You don't shave,' Morrissey pointed out mildly.

'I know but I like the smell, and if I've got it on nobody will know for certain.'

'Only a spot,' his father cautioned.

'Thanks, Dad!' He picked up the woggle. 'Where'd you find this?'

'It's evidence, Mike, put it down.'

'Evidence of what?'

Good question, thought Morrissey. What *was* the woggle evidence of?

'I don't know yet, it's something I have to find out.'

Michael squinted at it. 'There you are, initials. Thought there would be, it's the only way to stop 'em being nicked.'

'Where?' Morrissey took it from his son's hand and peered at it, turning it over and seeing nothing but scratches.

'You need specs, Dad. Look, IP and a seven.'

It could be, Morrissey thought. A microscope would settle it one way or the other, but since Michael was looking pleased with himself and eager for praise, he said thank you.

'No trouble, Dad. Anytime you're stuck.' He ducked Morrissey's pretend blow and went out.

At his office the chief inspector remembered to take the leather fastener out of his pocket, and had it on the desk in front of him when he rang Charlie Cotton's headmaster. He had toyed with the idea of ringing the previous night, but had thought a final, undisturbed sleep would do the boy more good.

There was an immediate, shocked silence at the other end of the line and then questions. 'This is terrible,' the headmaster said when he realised how bad things were. 'I don't know how to approach such a thing at all. One parent is bad enough, but both...'

'I hoped you might have the grandparents' addresses,' Morrissey said gently. 'If not, perhaps you could get them from Charlie before you break the news. Quite apart from them being able to help him, I shall need to speak to them myself, and it will be easier on the boy if the police are kept out of it at the moment. I'll ring you back in an hour, if you don't mind.'

When he had hung up, Morrissey found a plastic packet and dropped the woggle inside. No shortage of fingerprints on that, he thought, with a fair measure of guilt, and dropped it into the OUT tray for forensic.

An impatience filled his mind, and with it an obscure feeling that someone was deftly manipulating strings. It was too fanciful but it wouldn't leave him.

Not done in anger but carefully planned, coldly executed. A cool psychopath; those had been the police surgeon's words.

He took the envelope folder from his desk drawer. As Barrett had said there were only household bills, non personal items; a fancy card from her hairdressers, another from a beautician. He looked at the wedding photograph; it showed a younger Marion, not quite so blonde, in an expensive cream suit and pink roses. And the man at her side: balding, paunchy, mid-fifties. A short marriage then; it was a long time since Idi Amin had ended it. Wondering if Walsh had got a trial or a quick bullet, he put it to one side; best send a copy to the Met and find out more about him.

Nothing else then? Yes there was. He shook the folder and a part used book of matches dropped out, shiny black and pink letters. *Cobblers*. He picked it up and looked at it thoughtfully. Had it been in a drawer, on a table, or where? The chief inspector got up and went to look for Pace.

The young constable reddened when Morrissey dropped the matches on his desk. 'Sorry, sir, I just thought they might be useful. Didn't seem like the usual sort of place for her to go.'

'Why not? Disco place is it?' There had been a crop of such places opening over the last eighteen months. Even the pubs were into it now.

'Not—um, not exactly, it's—um,' Pace looked apologetic. 'It's a poofters' bar.'

Poofter! So much for progress and lectures on community policing. 'A homosexual meeting place,' Morrissey amended. 'You'll know where it is then?'

'On Middlebrook Road, near the Arts Centre.'

'Thanks. And it was good thinking to pick this up.' Morrissey retrieved the matches. 'In a drawer were they, or on a table?'

'In her handbag; well, one of them anyway. She had six. This one was in the sitting-room behind a chair cushion. I think it's probably the bag she'd been using that day; it matched her shoes. Ruth always reckons that's important.'

'Ruth is your wife?'

'Yes, sir.'

'She doesn't mind you policing?' It wasn't an idle question for Morrissey. So many police wives disliked and resented their husbands' work. Not surprising perhaps, but not comfortable to live with either, and if Pace wanted to move up it had to be right for him at home.

'No, sir, not yet, sir.'

Not yet, Morrissey mused as he went for his car. Did Pace think there would be a time when she would? Perhaps there was something in the American idea of interviewing wives before employing husbands.

He drove past *Cobblers* once without seeing it, but coming back slowly found it occupied a basement beneath a bookmaker's shop, its name not noticeable unless you were looking for it.

The chief inspector had expected something more glaring, and probably twee, but recognised that preconception could be put down to prejudice just as much as Pace's misnomer. There was a half arched window of amber coloured glass with the name across it in black lettering. Through the glass could be seen boothed tables and a bar hung with glasses. If he didn't know better he would probably think it just another wine bar.

Then he saw a waiter in small white bib and dicky-bow, and brief black shorts and knew he wouldn't. It took courage, he found, to go in.

Did he look like a policeman?

The slim young man with hair that curled like that of Michelangelo's *David* didn't seem to think so. Standing behind the bar he too wore a dicky-bow, but thankfully with a white shirt.

'Yes, *sir*, what can I get you? Haven't been here before have you? *Nice* place, you'll like it.' He eyed Morrissey disconcertingly.

'I'm not a customer,' the chief inspector said. 'I want to see the owner.'

'That's a pity. Personal then. *Lucky* Mr Wellen.' He smiled regretfully and called through a hatch behind the bar. 'Lennie? Lennie dear, if you've got a minute there's a *gentleman*.' He turned back to Morrissey. 'Won't be long. Have a glass of wine while you're waiting.'

'No thanks, too early.'

'Cup of coffee then. Won't take a minute.'

'Nothing,' said Morrissey looking round. Two booths were occupied; one couple were holding hands, the other pair looked bored. At the side of the bar a bead curtain, circa nineteen-sixties, rattled faintly as Wellen came through, his hair close cut and a small gold hoop in one ear; incongruous on the round face and low forehead. A black and silver waistcoat sat uneasily open over his paunch.

'That'll do, Derek. Find something to occupy yourself,' he said sharply. Then to Morrissey, 'He's young and can't tell the difference yet.' His eyes were busy examining the chief inspector's clothes. 'And you're not a salesman.'

'I'm a police officer,' said Morrissey and held up his warrant card. Wellen took a step back.

'For God's sake don't flash that in here. You'd better come through.' He turned back through the bead curtain and Derek's eyes followed them jealously.

Wellen obviously lived on the premises. A single window, high on the back wall and barred on the outside, let in too little light, and the room itself was all black and chrome; low tables, soft settees. One big, multi-coloured painting in a vaguely familiar style hung against a stark white wall. Nothing cheap. The bar must do well.

'It's a Pollock,' Wellen said over-anxiously. 'I snapped it up before the arty folk took him to their bosom. It's all quite legal, and the licence is up to date. I can't think what we've done wrong.'

Not long ago everything about the place would have been wrong Morrissey thought, but not since the repeal of the homosexuality laws. Prejudice died hard.

'Did I say anything was wrong?' he said. 'I just want to ask a few questions.' He took the book of matches from his pocket. 'Is this one of yours?'

'Yes. Bit of goodwill and advertising. Free of course.'

'You give out a lot?'

'Fair number.'

'And only to. . .' Morrissey felt himself balk at the word. . .'men?'

'Well we do get the odd lezzy in, not many though, wish we did.'

'What about a tall blonde, late thirties, smart, very sexy, throaty voice?'

'I'd remember *her*. I mean I might not want to go to bed with them but you don't have to be a vegetarian to like salads.'

'She could have come in for a drink by mistake.'

'I doubt it. Must have got it from a gentleman friend. We do have a few benders.'

And that would be much more of a blackmail proposition.

Morrissey made up his mind to send Barrett back with photographs.

He walked across the room. There were photographs here, displayed on the window wall, and although their content had been hard to distinguish in the half light, now he looked more closely he saw they were of boys, some clothed, some nude. And some definitely under age. All were homo-erotic. Wellen was almost wringing his hands.

'Art studies,' he said. 'You can see that from the background.'

'One man's art is another man's pornography,' Morrissey said. 'Some of these are borderline.'

'Surely not.' Panicking. 'They're just something beautiful to look at. You have the Pirelli calendar, I have these.'

Morrissey said, 'The Pirelli models aren't under age.'

'Oh that! Danish. Much more enlightened on the continent.'

'This is still England. If I had reason to believe you and your barman didn't keep strictly to the laws governing under-age drinking...' Morrissey began gravely, and Wellen interrupted.

'Nothing like that. No, no, of course! I don't want to lose my licence. There's nothing like that goes on here, Chief Inspector; not since I took over.'

'And I'm positive you'll remember to keep it that way. I'll want you to look at some photographs later today; it's possible there might be one you can recognise.'

'Anything I can do to help the police...' Morrissey recognised the note of relief. Why did everyone use the same words?

A gay bar, a book of matches, and Marion Walsh; somehow all three fitted together and the chief inspector exercised his mind with the problem of how as he drove back through Malminster.

Barrett was in the office and arguing on the telephone. 'Yes, I know these things are confidential but this is a murder inquiry. Then I'll come down and see you personally. Yes. Yes, an hour will be fine.' He put the receiver down sharply and looked at his senior officer; his eyes were annoyed and his face pink.

'Problems?' said Morrissey.

'Moxon's bank manager. Cagey as hell!'

'You'll persuade him. How did you get on with Goddard?'

Barrett shook his head. He had got back to the office missing Morrissey by a few minutes, and had felt disgruntled ever since. He had waited vainly for an

hour at Goddard's office and the architect hadn't
appeared.

Now he said bluntly, 'I didn't. He didn't show, and
nobody seems to know where the hell he is. Or at
least,' he amended, 'if they do no one is admitting it.
I rang his home.' He looked defensively at Morrissey. 'Mrs Goddard said he wasn't there. I thought I'd
better wait until you got back before I went to see her.'

'You think she might not be telling the truth?'

'Wives have been known to cover for their husbands before, and she might know where he was yesterday.'

'Not at his office?'

'Not according to his secretary. He left about
eleven; no one's seen him since. She's had to turn cli-
ents away and he's broken three appointments.' The
chief inspector watched him struggle. 'He fits the
picture, sir. Opportunity, access to cyanide, the only
one we didn't find anything to incriminate because he
had removed everything that could.' He waited to be
told he was wrong, quite certain of being right.

Instead Morrissey told him, 'Send out an alert just
in case. Airports, seaports, the usual; and find out if
he's made any large withdrawal from his bank account. I'll see Mrs Goddard myself. We'll probably
need to search the house again.'

How did you explain a hunch to a pragmatist sergeant who believed he had a clear-cut solution?

He dropped into his chair and looked at the neat
pile of computer print-outs on his desk. Information

was starting to come in now and would continue to do so. And somewhere among it would be an answer—or the beginning of an answer.

If he could find it.

Robert Goddard's absence niggled him. It didn't fit in with what he expected. Goddard was a part of things certainly, but there was something else, infinitely evil, and Morrissey felt that he could almost see it. And almost wasn't good enough.

SEVENTEEN

MORRISSEY SAID, 'I've already told the technician what I want. And wait for them, don't take any messing about. I want them back on my desk in an hour or less.'

'Sir!' Pace had on his eager puppy look. The envelope he held was sealed, but its contents would raise a few eyebrows in the photo lab. That was something that couldn't be helped; Morrissey wanted Wellen and his bartender to look at faces and not be distracted by what else was on view.

The chief inspector tried to remember at what point eagerness died. Was it simply a matter of age or a steady process of being stamped on?

He pulled the telephone towards him. Much more than an hour had gone since he had spoken to young Charlie Cotton's headmaster. It was now well into the school morning. But he could give slightly better news about Cotton senior, who had shown a small overnight improvement. That might take the edge off Charlie's fears.

'I'm sorry,' the headmaster said stiffly, 'but I'm afraid I made contact with the grandparents myself. Charles is insistent that he return home, and I must make quite certain he is cared for there; after all he is my responsibility. Only his paternal grandparents are living, and they are travelling from Cheadle to be with their grandson.'

'To the school?'

'To the school, and then on to Malminster.'

And the round journey would take the most part of a day. Little chance of speaking to them before tomorrow, but he gave the telephone number of Malminster CID, and his personal extension, and asked for them to be passed on.

On his desk the neat stack of papers could be ignored no longer; he discovered there had been a plethora of prints in the Walsh house. Obviously no daily had meant no dusting.

Moxon, whether he liked it or not, would have to press his well manicured fingers onto the inky slab. Cotton's and Goddard's were already on file, but there were Mrs Cotton's to be got, and soon.

The autopsy report itself made grisly reading.

A compressed fracture of the left temporal bone had extended mid-way into the parietal; the blow forceful enough to rupture brain tissue and cause extensive damage. It had also fractured the left cheek bone. Death would have followed quickly even without the mutilating gashes.

The coldly clinical lines confirmed Reed's hypothesis that the initial blow had been delivered by someone facing her, someone tall enough and heavy enough to exert extreme force.

Not Mrs Cotton then, despite forensic confirmation that the stains on her clothing belonged to Marion Walsh's blood-group. But she had been there at or about the time of the murder, that was clear. What was unclear was why. And, even more importantly, what had she seen that was locked, unreachable, in her brain?

He scowled, knowing he mustn't waste his time with it until after a psychiatric assessment had been done; and God knew how long that would take. Impatiently he turned to bitty, preliminary reports from the Met that held nothing really useful yet. Fact: most murders were committed by family members or close friends, yet here were two dead women in Little Henge seemingly without either.

Barrett came back, frustration still uppermost, and the feeling intensified when Morrissey told him to collect Mrs Cotton's fingerprints. His face took on a frozen look. Why all this when he had Goddard almost nailed?

Morrissey felt his sergeant's resentment and said mildly, 'Won't take you long. Plenty of time before you go to the bank. And when you've finished there,' a smile, briefly apologetic, 'get over to Moxon's and ask him politely to come back here with you and put his on file.'

'He could get stroppy.'

'He could, but you'll not let a little thing like that stand in your way, will you?' Morrissey said obliquely, and rubbed in a little salt. 'I'm going to have a talk with Mrs Goddard, ask if she knows where her husband is.'

Barrett bridled. 'Sir, I...'

'Think I'm taking it off your plate, don't you? Well, I'm not. When you've passed me on the ladder we'll do it the other way round.'

Barrett knew what his thoughts were but decided against verbalising them. Middle-aged men were vulnerable to attractive women; something to do with a need to prove they could still pull a bird—he remembered reading that somewhere, but it wasn't the sort of thing to bring up with the chief.

Morrissey lifted an interrogative eyebrow.

'I'm going,' Barrett said, picking up his jacket.

Morrissey watched the door close, and asked himself: If Robert Goddard were lying low, where would he go? Not back to his home unless he thought his wife would be completely loyal, and could even an egoist such as he believed Goddard to be expect that?

It was a question that remained unanswered as he drove to the village.

He turned into the Community Centre and parked. There was a Ford transit near the single storey building and a group of people around it. A banner on the side nearest to Morrissey read: HANDS OFF OUR VILLAGE—WE DON'T WANT YOUR RUBBISH. He wandered across. 'What's all this, then?'

There were hostile looks. A woman with a T-shirt that said aggressively, *Up Yours*, responded. 'It means we don't want your bloody rubbish down our

quarry, that's what,' she said, and they all piled into
the back of the van. He watched it drive off towards
Malminster.

Blake was missing from the operations room and a
sergeant from communications had taken his place.
Apologetic without reason, he said the inspector had
been sent to control a mid-week cup-tie that threatened trouble. 'Most of the men have been taken off
too,' he added. 'Noises from the top.'

Morrissey shrugged philosophically, knowing the
biggest part of the foot-work had been completed. If
nothing had turned up so far, chances were nothing
would. Little Henge was an insular place, and more
so now it had lost its chief gossip.

He said, 'Any idea what the natives are going to
war about?'

The sergeant grinned. 'The council want to fill up
the old quarry, and they're not best pleased.'

Morrissey thought about the constant flow of tip-
per trucks that would thunder through the village and
understood why. He drove slowly to the Goddard
house. It was now almost noon and there were few
people about, those who were seeming impervious to
the fact that he was a stranger despite the village having had two violent deaths in as many days. The exception was the flapping figure in black. Did he
always wear a cassock?

Morrissey pulled up and got out of the car, waiting until the vicar drew level.

Bartholomew had been walking down Vicarage Lane, mid-way between the allotment path and his home, with carrots in one hand and a cabbage balanced on the other.

'From the allotment of one of my older parishioners,' he said. 'I'm afraid every time he sees me walking past he feels he must contribute to my table. It was a very bad business yesterday. I'm sorry I wasn't on hand, but unfortunately it was my day for visiting in Stenton. Are you making any progress, Chief Inspector?'

'It's early days, Vicar, but things are coming together slowly. I'd like to find someone who saw Mrs Hartley after she left the Walsh house.'

Bartholomew said easily, 'I did, Chief Inspector. Mrs Cator at number nine is bedridden and I take Communion to her. I saw Mrs Hartley letting herself into her home about—let's see—just before one?'

'And you spoke to her.'

'Briefly; she said she was expecting a friend to drop in and hadn't time to talk.'

'But you didn't think to tell me before?'

'You didn't ask me,' the vicar said reasonably, 'and it didn't seem important.'

'It would if she'd said who the friend was.'

'But she didn't, Chief Inspector, and therefore it isn't any help, is it? It will be good when it's over and the village can renew itself. Can I offer you lunch?'

'I think not. But I may come and see you again before long. I'm sure there are other things you might help me with.'

'Anytime, always providing it doesn't entail breaking a confidence.'

'If a man came to you today,' said Morrissey, 'with this on his conscience, would you protect innocence or preserve guilt?'

Bartholomew shook his head. 'I think that might come under the category of a loaded question, but I will, I promise, give it some thought.'

As he walked away, Morrissey was conscious again of a sense of alienation. Was it antipathy to Bartholomew himself or to the inflexible dogma behind him?

In the arched porch of the Goddard house the chief inspector found himself hesitating. Given provocation to extreme anger, he believed Goddard, like the majority of people, would be capable of murder. What he didn't believe, despite Barrett's conviction to the contrary, was that Goddard was the type to cold bloodedly *plan* to kill.

Now if Goddard didn't turn up with a satisfactory account of his movements this house would have to be searched again, and this time much more thoroughly. It was an idea that troubled him. He had given the order to search so many houses without a second thought, but now his mind pushed the knowledge forcibly into his consciousness that Helen Goddard would loathe to have her home turned over by police fingers, down to the smallest and most intimate of possessions. Annoyed that he might be letting emotion colour judgement, he pressed the bell. If it was necessary he would give the order again, here.

The door opened quickly, as if she had been standing waiting for the ring of the bell. Skilful make-up gave a bloom to Helen Goddard's face, but the dark shadows were still there. Despite that she seemed glad to see him.

'Come in,' she said, standing back. 'I've been expecting you.'

He stepped past her and stood in the hall, her perfume fanning back towards him as she closed the door. He should have brought a WPC with him, but it was the last thing he wanted to do, and he felt like an adolescent.

'I have to ask about...'

'Robert,' she said, cutting in. 'Yes, I know, your sergeant rang earlier.' She walked into the sitting-room and he followed her. 'He isn't here, but if you want to look for him you can. He didn't come home last night.'

'Were you surprised?'

'Yes. Not perhaps that he should want to be away, to have thinking time, but Robert is fairly fastidious, and would have wanted a change of clothing, his toiletries.'

'He couldn't have collected them without you knowing?'

'No. I went out only for a few minutes yesterday, to the post-box at the bottom of the hill. There wouldn't have been time. Will you have some coffee, Chief Inspector? I should like some myself so it really won't be a trouble. If you're worried I might be slipping away to warn Robert you can come into the kitchen while I make it. But then,' she made a small dismissive gesture, 'come anyway, the sun is on the back of the house and we can take it outside, it's such a lovely day.'

The words were a jolt. Half the day had gone and he hadn't consciously noticed the sun was out. Now he followed her into the kitchen and saw it streaming through the window.

'What time did you go out to the post?' he said, leaning against the door jamb, watching her.

She didn't answer immediately, but instead busied herself with the filter machine.

'What time did Mrs Walsh die?' she said eventually, and glanced at him sideways. 'That isn't fair, is it? About a quarter past twelve, I suppose. The post-box is emptied at half-past, and yesterday the van was too early and the driver went into the post office to wait. Martha made him a pot of tea.'

'You went in too?'

'For a fresh loaf of bread.'

'Did you see anyone else?'

'Old Willie, walking up to his allotment, a couple of young mums with push-chairs going up the hill. I remember they were laughing and it made me think how I used to be when the children were small.'

'Anyone else?' he said gently.

She shook her head. 'I don't think so. Can you pass me two mugs from the cupboard at the side of you? Thanks. There were a few men outside the Black Bull but I didn't know them. Black?'

'Half an inch of milk, no sugar. How did you know about Mrs Walsh?' he said as she passed him a mug. 'If that was the only time you went out, who told you about her death?'

'Well, the grape-vine isn't entirely dormant,' she said, opening the outside door. 'So I could say I found out that way, but it wouldn't be the truth.' She waited until he lowered himself onto the other garden chair, and then leaned back with closed eyes, letting the sun play full on her face. 'Sergeant Barrett told me this morning, Chief Inspector. I gather that's why you're looking for Robert.'

Her hand was on the arm of her chair and he had an urge to cover it with his own. Would the action comfort her as it would Margaret? Guilt came and he brought his mind sharply back to what she had said.

He sighed. There was no reason why Barrett shouldn't have told her; it would have been fair to assume she would have heard by then. In fact it could be argued that instead of chasing up Turner and Moxon, he should have come here. But if he had Robert Goddard wouldn't have been here, waiting for him.

Morrissey stared at a cluster of midges dancing in a pool of shade and tried to work out the probability Helen was lying.

She asked calmly, 'How did she die?' There was no curiosity in her voice, it was just a question, and when she sat forward and looked at him she knew immediately that he couldn't tell her. 'I'm sorry, I don't need to know; I don't really *want* to know. But if it were Robert it would have to be a very tidy death, he always passes out at the sight of blood. Some people do, you know.'

Morrissey thought about that on his way back to Malminster. A very tidy death. But it had been a very lively form of death, and not tidy at all.

Pace had left the photographs on the chief inspector's desk, not studio prints by a long way, but recognisable.

Turner, Moxon, Cotton and Marion Walsh. He added a snapshot of Robert Goddard that Helen had provided, and when Barrett returned a few minutes later gave them to him. The sergeant's resentment was palpable. He dropped a thick, brown envelope on Morrissey's desk.

'Details of Moxon's bank account,' he said. 'I called in at Goddard's office again. He still hasn't come in.'

'He'll turn up sooner or later,' said the chief inspector, 'but in the meantime let's see if anybody at *Cobblers* can connect with one or more of those faces. And, Neil,' he said as Barrett turned away, 'we're paid to detect. Let's get on with it, shall we? There's no solid evidence one way or the other and there won't be if we don't turn it up. Bear that in mind.'

'I thought I was doing, sir,' Barrett answered stiffly, and wished his chief would do the same instead of chasing dead ends. If *he* were in charge of the investigation he'd pull out all the stops to find Goddard; anything else was a waste of time.

EIGHTEEN

As FAR AS Morrissey was concerned it was a day that staggered from one wasted journey to the next.

It didn't help when the consultant psychiatrist gave a firm "no" to the idea of questioning Mrs Cotton, pointing out that mentally she was twelve years old, and everything that had happened to her since had been blocked out. 'And don't ask me how long for,' he added; 'it could be a week, it could be a year.'

Then Barrett drew a blank at the wine bar and Morrissey's sense of frustration threatened to boil over.

'I didn't really expect anything,' Barrett said gloomily. 'And even if they'd picked out Goddard, it would have been a bit of an overkill. He hasn't shown up yet, I suppose?' There was something in the way he said it that got beneath the chief inspector's skin. Barrett waited, and when nothing was forthcoming said tentatively, 'Think we should look around the house again?'

Morrissey stared at him thoughtfully. There were times when the sergeant became too bumptious for his own good. He looked at his watch. 'You can bring me a ham sandwich back from the canteen. And coffee. Better get down there before they sell out.'

Barrett's lips pursed in disapproval. 'It wouldn't hurt to apply for a warrant,' he said stiffly.

'Now,' Morrissey suggested gently, adding, 'I wouldn't want you to go hungry two days on the trot. Low blood sugar disturbs logical thinking.'

Barrett turned on his heel and fretted to himself about immovability. They were getting nowhere, and in the meantime Goddard was slipping away to ground. He debated the pleasure of being able to say, ultimately: I told you so, and found it a sweet thought.

IT WAS almost eleven when Morrissey gave up trying to make sense of the papers and reports on his desk. The Met had sent a pile of FAX sheets that laid open Marion Walsh's life up to her marriage. It didn't make pretty reading; a mother finding punters for her by the time she was twelve; an abortion at thirteen and then a care order, revoked by some idiot two years later. He calculated mentally and decided she'd still been under sixteen when she hit the skin magazines.

A long list of pornographic films was attached. User and used; where did one end and the other begin?

And then she married. Morrissey fished out the wedding photograph again. Had her husband known? Had he wanted Marion or a porno star? The chief inspector put the papers away and went home.

Under all the too-pale make-up, his own daughter was already a feminist and for the first time Morrissey felt glad about it.

Margaret was still up, wholesome and sleepy in dressing gown and slippers. Morrissey wondered what had kept her there, waiting. They had long ago established a routine whereby she left a flask of soup and a plate of sandwiches when he worked late. There were larks and owls and he was a bit of both, but Margaret was wholly lark. A sudden fear came that it might be to do with Michael or Katie.

He gave her a quick peck on the cheek.

'Something up?'

'I'll put the kettle on and make some coffee,' she said, 'then I can talk while you eat.'

She padded into the kitchen and he followed.

'Sounds serious.' He took off his jacket and draped it over the back of a chair. 'Kids?'

'Not ours.' She watched him wash his hands. 'Do you want coffee or just soup? It's instant.'

'Soup'll do fine. Whose then?' He took the cling film from the plate of sandwiches and sat down. 'Committee meeting?' There had been times in the past when some aspect of the NSPCC's work had upset her.

She brought her coffee to the table. 'We got talking about missing children. It isn't all crisis intervention now, you know, there's more emphasis on prevention and counselling, but...' She was frowning, trying to find a way to express what was really half formed disquiet. 'What makes the difference,' she said finally, 'between putting a child down as a runaway or pulling out all the stops and treating it as ... as ... ?'

'Possible child murder. That's what you're asking, isn't it?' Morrissey wished she hadn't brought it up now, he was tired and wanted nothing more than to eat his supper in peace and go to bed, but he knew the fact that she had waited up made it important to her. Perhaps there was more to be said; rumours she'd decided he should hear, so he chewed thoughtfully and in his mind went over those things that would act as significators for him. A note perhaps; a schoolfriend told of intention, possessions packed and gone, savings drawn out of the post office; sometimes money stolen because the runaway had none. He tried to explain all these things and then waited for what was to come.

When it did it brought a frisson of surprise that Margaret had amassed such facts at one committee meeting; gathering strands, weaving them into a disturbing whole. Why hadn't he known, why hadn't some bright spark in the division added up the numbers and dropped it onto someone's desk for a look-see?

Eight youngsters in and around Malminster had left home in less than two years. Statistically improbable, disturbing if true. Something Barrett could find out. Now he asked, 'Not just rumours?'

'There's a list,' his wife fished in her dressing gown pocket. 'I said I'd tell you. It was only tonight when we were talking... I don't think anyone had added them up before.'

'What brought it up?'

She frowned at him. 'Me. I was asking around for news of the boy from Mike's school; you know, Philip Duffin. And then these names kept coming up. What will you do?'

'I'll look into it.' It was a promise and satisfied her. 'Might have to wait until the present job is over,' he qualified, 'but it won't get put away and forgotten.'

There was warmth in her eyes and smile. Morrissey counted himself lucky. And then, unexpectedly, thought of Helen Goddard and felt ashamed, as if the thought in itself were a part betrayal.

HE WAS DREAMING, wrapped in that last, deep sleep before waking. He knew the dream was complex and that there were threads he wanted to remember, but as always as soon as his eyes opened the dream dissolved. It was a quarter to seven, almost the time he would normally have woken, and the telephone was sending out a high pitched warble. Not for the first time Morrissey regretted the passing of the old, squat model with its honest-to-God ring muted at night under a tea-cosy. This new, slim instrument might be sleeker but he hated its chirruping.

He lifted the receiver and said, 'Morrissey,' and listened without speaking until the other voice was silent. Then he said, 'Let Detective Sergeant Barrett know, and tell him I'll meet him there.' When he hung up Margaret was awake.

'Problems?'

'I don't know yet.' He grimaced. 'Today could be the day I finally get proved wrong.'

'I'll make coffee while you shave.' She slid out of bed and reached for her dressing gown.

'Nothing to eat,' he warned. 'There isn't time.' She smiled at him and went out. By the time he had shaved, the smell of coffee mixed with that of bacon had brought a quick flow of gastric juices. When he went downstairs his wife was folding a sandwich into a paper towel and handed it to him as he took a quick gulp of coffee.

'Eat and drive,' she commanded. 'It'll stop you going too fast.'

'I never go too fast,' he lied and bent to kiss her.

STONEY LANE was on the north side of Malminster, deeply rutted and leading nowhere except to a fenced off and disused quarry. On its way it cut through a corner of Brindley Woods, hiding dark underneath the trees at night and because of that a favourite spot for courting couples. It was possible, with care, to drive off the road and into the trees; Robert Goddard had done that.

And afterwards, it seemed, he had decided to kill himself.

NINETEEN

BARRETT HAD THE appearance of a sparky cockerel and although he had the sense not to crow out loud, Morrissey had no trouble recognising the thick layer of self-satisfaction. He would probably have been the same if their positions had been reversed, counting it a feather in his cap to be right and a senior officer wrong. And still there was a niggle at the back of the chief inspector's mind that wouldn't lie down and die.

The cyanide bottle in the well of the car near Goddard's feet had held only the dead man's fingerprints, that had been the first thing Morrissey had checked. And there had been a note of sorts in his left hand. Brief. Too brief in fact. The words "I'm sorry" scrawled on a page ripped out of his pocket diary. Did that fit with what he knew of Goddard's character? Helen hadn't been sure, but he hadn't expected her to be, faced by the circumstances of her husband's death. Then a thorough search of the house and garden had turned up a pair of rubber gloves that still had traces of Marion Walsh's blood on them.

'You can buy them anywhere,' Morrissey had growled. 'Why would he leave the damn things in a garden shed? Instinct would have made him get rid of them.'

'No point,' Barrett said cheerfully, 'if he was going to top himself.'

Morrissey wasn't happy when the hierarchy came to the same conclusion as the detective sergeant, that the gloves provided the final knot to tie the case up tight, but he had to live with the fact that apart from concluding formalities, such as a formal inquest, the case was closed to everyone's satisfaction but his own.

The chief inspector was in the churchyard when Betty Hartley was buried on a cool, gusty day, with flurries of rain alternating with brief bursts of watery sun. There were few mourners, but at least there were some. Her son, solemnly uncomfortable and alone, had his eyes fixed at some point distant to the churchyard. Remembering good times or bad, Morrissey wondered, and half wished he had access to the other's thoughts. William Hartley had shown shock but not grief when he learned about his mother's death, yet some lingering emotional tie had remained to bring him here; or was it duty alone that bridged the years of silence? Apart from him there was just the bird-like woman from the post office, and Ida Hodge with her husband, her eyes darting from one face to another, missing nothing.

Morrissey stood some distance back, half hidden by tall elders; but Ida had seen him almost at once. It wouldn't be long, the chief inspector decided, before she took on Betty's mantle. He caught the faint rattle of earth on wood and knew it was almost over. Bartholomew closed his prayer book and spoke to the son, who stood stolidly and seemed not to respond. Ida turned away, threading between graves towards the chief inspector.

'Didn't think you'd bother to turn up,' she said. 'Not with that Goddard man settling everything up like he did.'

Like a debt, Morrissey thought, paid in full; life at its simplest. But Goddard hadn't been tried and hadn't been found guilty, not by judge and jury, only by the act of closing a file.

As if she hadn't expected him to answer her, Ida talked on, her satisfaction shining like a dark halo. 'I could hear poor Betty turning in her grave, you know, listening to all that said over her and not being able to answer back. Couldn't have kept quiet if she'd been alive.'

The wry thought came to Morrissey that if she'd been alive she wouldn't have needed to. 'I didn't hear what was said,' he pointed out.

'Wasn't what was said,' Ida came back triumphantly, 'but who said it. Betty didn't fancy him at all. Said to me, "Ida," she says, "you'll not get me in that place again while he's there, not ever." Never did tell me what they'd had words about, though,' she said regretfully.

Morrissey thought that gossip had probably been one factor, and said as much. Ida sniffed.

'Betty never said nothing that wasn't true, and you can't blame her for the way certain people carry on.'

'No,' said Morrissey, 'but sometimes it's best to let things stay hidden; less hurtful in the long run, and certainly less fatal.'

'I could tell you something else about that too, but there's not much point now, is there?' She squinted up at him. 'Unless you asked me like.'

Morrissey sighed; he might as well ask and get rid of her that way. Once she'd discharged her batteries she'd go back to where her husband stood looking at them uneasily. He looked at the plain, pudgy face before him. 'Tell me,' he encouraged. 'What is it I don't already know?'

'Well, that Robert Goddard never poisoned that milk.' Her hand fastened on his elbow, and he caught a whiff of halitosis as she leaned confidentially forward. 'Couldn't have. He passed my Edwin on the road in that flashy car of his, and Ned hadn't done his delivery then. What d'you make of that then, eh?'

Morrissey stared back at her, feeling the nudge of cold unreason, and knew that if Ida wasn't lying, a killer had got away with three, near perfect, murders.

TWENTY

'LET IT LIE, John,' said the head of CID. 'This milk-man, Hodge or whatever, probably mistook the day. The case has been closed and I don't see any need to resurrect it. Sorry.'

Morrissey was sorry too. Sorry there were so many ends he didn't think had been tied off neatly enough. The extra concentration of cyanide in the Hartley woman's cup for one. That hadn't been explained and now probably never would be.

'Get back to me if anything else turns up,' the chief superintendent said, 'and I'll look at it again.' It was an offer without much substance but he hoped it would pacify Morrissey.

Perversity rather than duty had taken the chief inspector to Betty Hartley's funeral, as it took him to Marion Walsh's cremation. The chapel was bare of people; the coffin empty except for one wreath. He sat at the back and waited. Eventually the coroner's officer came in, saw Morrissey, and sat beside him.

'It's the devil, isn't it? I hate these jobs where nobody turns up; it scares the hell out of me. No relatives?'

'There might be a mother somewhere if she's still alive. I'm not sure it wouldn't have been an insult to her daughter if she'd come.'

'That bad?'

'Worse,' said Morrissey and meant it. Whatever Marion Walsh had done could only be a part payment back on what had been done to her. But it wasn't in his brief to find excuses; if she had lived he would have tried to prove blackmail and not weighed the fine balance of morality.

Someone turned the music up; more like Musak, Morrissey thought. Beside him, the other man moved uncomfortably. 'Someone should say something.' It was a protest and the chief inspector wondered if Bartholomew ought to have been told.

'Who's the wreath from?' he asked. 'Any idea?'

'Her solicitors. It'll come out of the estate.'

Morrissey winced.

His companion complained, 'They were supposed to be sending a representative from the office. Should do, considering how much they'll collect in fees.'

And who would get the estate? That was another end not tied up. As the thought came, a side door opened to let in two men. One was Bartholomew, the other wasn't known to Morrissey.

Beside him, the coroner's man was visibly relieved. 'That's him,' he said. 'He must have picked up the priest on his way here.'

At least someone had thought of it. Would Marion Walsh have approved, or would she have laughed out loud? Somehow Morrissey thought it would have been the second. He half expected Bartholomew to stand behind the lectern and offer platitudes, but that didn't happen. Instead he bent his head near the coffin and said a brief prayer. When it ended the curtains closed without any further waiting, and the doors behind hissed slightly as they opened.

Morrissey waited outside to ask the question uppermost in his mind. The solicitor seemed surprised the chief inspector was still interested.

'The National Children's Home gets the lot,' he said indifferently. 'Not what I would expect from such a source, but no doubt she had her reasons.'

'Yes,' Morrissey agreed, remembering. 'She had.'

Bartholomew was standing close, listening, and the chief inspector supposed that having arrived with the solicitor he was waiting to be taken home by him too. He seemed put out.

'That was an area of Mrs Walsh's life I knew nothing about,' he said vexedly. 'What a pity you didn't mention it on the way here. I could have said something about her good works during the service.'

'Hardly a service,' the solicitor said stiffly.

Morrissey said, 'It must be difficult finding things to say. There can't be more than a handful of people in the parish you know well enough to be honest about.'

'A little more than that chief inspector, but the circumstances are usually less complicated.'

'They'll be complicated when it comes to Robert Goddard's turn too,' Morrissey said. 'Are suicides still excluded?'

'No one is excluded, God's forgiveness is without limit just as all things are ordained by Him.'

'Even murder?' asked Morrissey.

'One of the Mysteries to ponder on,' said Bartholomew. 'I only wish I had time to debate it, but I have a confirmation class in fifteen minutes.'

Morrissey watched the two men walk to the solicitor's car, and knew that for the third time he had failed to pin Bartholomew down.

HE WENT HOME EARLY. Margaret was out and the house felt empty. When his son came in from school Morrissey remembered the promise she had exacted and felt vexation at a week allowed to pass without doing anything about it.

Mike said cheerfully, 'Hi, Dad, I'm knackered,' and slung his school bag into the corner behind the kitchen door. 'Don't fancy a bit of maths homework, do you?'

Morrissey wondered what pressures would make Mike run from his home. There were glue sniffers at his comprehensive school; not many but enough to cause talk, and last year rumours of soft drugs had reached Morrissey's ears. To protect without being overbearing was a constant worry; so far they seemed to have managed, he and Margaret together. But suppose . . . just suppose either Mike or Katie . . . He snapped his mind away from the unthinkable.

'If you don't mind wrong answers,' he said equably.

His son opened the fridge. 'Think Mum would miss half a chicken?'

'She might,' Morrissey acknowledged, 'but she usually forgives small sins. Mike, I want you to talk to me about Philip Duffin. Everything you can think of from graffiti in the lavatory to what he ate for lunch. And if you're thinking of eating, get your hands washed.'

'You know what Gran says: "Everyone's got to eat a peck of dirt."'

'Not all at once.'

Mike went to the sink. 'He was a bit of a wimp,' he said as he turned on the tap, 'teachers nark.' He squinted sideways at his father. 'Good at running, useless at football, dead timid. I don't reckon he ran away at all really. Don't think he'd got the bottle. Maybe his old man done him in, he didn't like him much.'

'What makes you say that?' Morrissey said sharply.

'Things get round,' Mike said uncomfortably. 'I don't know if they're true or not. Only. . .'

'Only what?'

'Only Stew Riley said Duffin's dad used to belt him.' He scowled, drying his hands.

'And how did Stew know?'

'Lives next door.' Mike reddened. 'I know I said Phil was a wimp but I didn't really mind him, and his dad was a right ugly sod!'

'Michael!'

'Sorry.' A shrug. 'Anyway he never made trouble, never had any tuck money, sang in the church choir, and kept falling asleep.' He looked at the grey patch where he had dried his hands and turned the towel so it didn't show. 'I don't know anything else,' he said. 'Is that enough?'

Morrissey put his jacket back on slowly. 'Yes,' he said. 'Yes, Mike it's plenty. If your mother says anything about the chicken, tell her I said it was all right.'

'Thanks.' He frowned at his father. 'You going back to work?'

'Not for long,' Morrissey said. 'Just something I want to do before morning.'

He met Margaret near the gate; she looked disappointed.

'I'll try not to be late,' he promised. 'Mike's home. I told him he could eat the cold chicken.'

'Forget the casserole then,' she said wryly.

He bent awkwardly and kissed her, knowing Mrs Peebles over the road was watching from her window. 'I'll talk to you later,' he said, and drove off without looking back.

The list of names got a critical look and a grumble about a lack of dates, which the chief inspector dismissed with a cutting edge to his tongue that silenced the duty sergeant. Morrissey knew that a lot of his anger stemmed from the case that had ended, for him, at an impasse; but there was anger too for what he suspected would prove to be a flaw in the system.

Tomorrow, if he was right, it would be sealed.

Barrett was on the point of leaving. There was a bottle of wine standing on his desk; not plonk, Morrissey noticed, but a good year. Having been proved right about Goddard, the sergeant no longer thought of his chief as omnipotent. But he was wary when Morrissey picked up the bottle.

'Something special, Neil?'

'Quiet meal unless something's up.'

'Nothing for you,' the chief inspector said. 'Not yet.' He put the wine on the desk. 'Enjoy your dinner. Anybody I know?'

Barrett was quick with his denial; not Janet Yarby then, if it were her he would have been boasting.

When the files came, three were marked closed; two fourteen-year-old girls had been found working in cafes on the south coast, one had been pregnant and both were now in care; a thirteen-year-old boy, parents divorced, had hitch-hiked to Wales to be with his father.

Bring him back and he'd run again. The boy's own words.

Four of the other five had made a habit of staying away from home for one night or more; a familiar pattern for runaways. Morrissey felt a frisson of surprise that Philip Duffin had been one of those; had a night in the open been less fearful than one at home to a boy known for his timidity?

The fifth file was already stamped CID. Reading it, Morrissey remembered the case vaguely. It had come up during his holidays—he'd been away a month and when he got back the initial impetus was dying down.

It had been Beckett's case, and Morrissey would need to ask before sticking his own nose in. However, handing the opportunist burglar Miller over to Beckett had made the inspector look good and left him owing Morrissey a favour. With that in mind, the chief inspector locked the files in his top drawer and turned out the light.

Pace was on duty at the front desk, and looked tired.

On his way out, Morrissey asked, 'Not sleeping?'

'Too much heavy traffic. Then there's noise from the comp.'

'Which?'

'Fisher.'

'Seen anybody lurking around there, chatting up kids?'

Pace's eyes lost their tiredness. 'No. Something going on?'

'Probably not,' said Morrissey. 'Worth keeping your eyes open though. Have you filled in that form yet?'

Pace nodded. CID Aide was a plum and he didn't think he had a hope, but he'd filled the form in; so had a few others.

'Should know soon,' said Morrissey turning away.
'It's likely to be quick.'

In which case, with three more weeks to do on
nights, he'd better forget about it, thought Pace.

Since his last visit to the wine bar the chief inspector had developed a habit of driving home past *Cobblers*, slowing to a crawl as he went by. He did that
now, winding his window down and catching the
sound of disco beating from the wide open door. He
thought he recognised two boys from Fisher daw-
dling on the pavement. The bar was less than two
hundred yards from the school, not a crime in itself
and probably less of a danger in some ways than a
rough pub... Even so it wouldn't do any harm to have
another word with Wellen about under-age drinking,
even if he had denied it once already.

Morrissey speeded up slightly, the late evening
traffic was still brisk. During the daytime, carrying
traffic from the motorway to Malminster and the
east, it was practically nose to tail along here. Not
much fun for Pace. He passed the school and
squinted to his left, knowing the young constable
rented a maisonette over a launderette. A little further along he pulled in to the kerb and turned off the
engine, tapping his fingers on the steering wheel.

He remembered the bottle of wine on Barrett's
desk, the sergeant's awkwardness with Pace, and the
raw nerve touched by a hypothetical question about
cuckolding.

A quiet dinner.

He walked back down the road and saw he hadn't been mistaken. It was Barrett's car.

TWENTY-ONE

MORRISSEY DEBATED with himself. He wasn't a guardian of morals and Barrett was off duty; plus which he had no direct knowledge that the sergeant *was* visiting Pace's flat, there were other flats nearby and several restaurants where he might be eating; the wine could well be for later. He looked up at the lighted windows, sensing odd looks from passers-by; the idea that he might be taken for a villain amused him.

After five minutes he got into his car to drive home, but at the roundabout, just before the turning into Forest Drive, the chief inspector changed his mind and returned to Middlebrook Road, knowing he could end up looking remarkably silly if Barrett wasn't there. But the risk would be better than losing a good sergeant.

The street door at the side of the launderette was locked; a sensible precaution. Morrissey kept his finger on the bell-push to a count of ten and then waited, stepping away from the door to let himself be seen from the upstairs window. When the door opened it was the detective sergeant and not Ruth Pace who faced him. Light came from an open door at the top of the steep flight of stairs; deliberately he made his voice loud.

'There's something important come up, Neil. Apologise to Mrs Pace for me. I'm sorry to drag you away.' Barrett looked shaken; he also looked indecisive. Morrissey wondered if Pace's wife were standing just out of sight, listening.

Barrett himself had a gut feeling that was neither sickness nor anger; more a cold knowledge that such a bad miscalculation could earn him a move he didn't want to make. The chief inspector's face was bland enough for him to be speaking the truth, but instinct told the sergeant otherwise. He shifted his weight and stayed silent.

'Off you go then,' Morrissey said inflexibly. 'I'll wait here.'

Barrett's head moved in resignation and he turned back up the stairs. The chief inspector didn't envy him. Pace's wife would be wondering who else knew where Barrett had been.

Sitting in the chief inspector's car Barrett said stiffly, 'It was quite innocent, nothing happened.'

'Dave Pace knows all about it then? I'm glad about that,' Morrissey looked at him. 'Otherwise one of you would have had to go.' Acerbically he added, 'I'd be sorry to lose you, Neil.'

Barrett fixed his eyes on the car headlights coming over the brow of the hill and felt a sense of aggrievement. Ruth had made the suggestion that if he brought wine she could provide food. Anything else had been left open. And the chief had no room to talk, the way he had bayed after the Goddard woman.

'I was invited.' It was a mistake and he knew it as soon as the words were out.

Morrissey stared at him impassively. ' "Lord, the woman tempted me and I did sin?" I'm surprised at you, Neil, if that's the best you can come up with. Is this the first time?'

'Yes.'

'Make sure there isn't a second.' Morrissey leaned across him and opened the door. 'I should go home if I were you.'

Barrett put one foot out on the pavement and sank his pride. 'Sorry, sir, it was a bad mistake. It won't happen again.'

'Glad to hear it. Come in early; there's a lot to do.' He turned the key in the ignition and Barrett got out hastily, standing at the kerb watching Morrissey's receding rear lights and wondering if tomorrow the warning would be made official. *Shit*! Without looking up at the lighted windows he got into his own car and drove away.

MORRISSEY WINCED. The chief superintendent had a habit of sucking air through his teeth when he was thinking. He did it now, drumming his fingers against the desk top and staring at the pile of files.

'Apart from the Pallister boy they follow the usual pattern,' he said finally. 'But you think there's too many?' He leaned back and looked at Morrissey, having learned to respect hunches that in anyone else he would have dismissed out of hand.

'Duffin is different too. Not on the surface maybe, but he was a timid boy with a violent father, and I tend to think the odd nights he slept rough were due to physical terror, not rebelliousness. And then there's the closeness of ages. Wouldn't you expect a wider spread? If they'd been girls the same age, pre-pubescent...'

Osgodby sucked harder. 'I can see the picture, John, thanks—and I hope to God you prove yourself wrong. Need more help?'

'Not yet. Later perhaps if there's something in it.'

'Keep me informed. I'll leave you to have a word with Beckett.' He handed the files back. 'At least you're not still worrying about the Walsh case.' His tone suggested humour but Morrissey didn't smile; the murders at Little Henge were still very much on his mind but there was no reason for Osgodby to know that.

Downstairs, waiting, Barrett wished he was busy. Usually the brief hiatus between cases was something to be looked forward to, but today he was practically praying for something to get him out of the office. Morrissey had told him to come in early, and he had, but when he'd asked where the chief inspector was and learned he was upstairs with the Super, his mind had leapt to warnings and transfer. He was still sweating about the idea when Morrissey came in.

'About last night...' Barrett began.

Morrissey cut him short. 'Last night we were both off duty, now we're not. Don't want to make it official, do you?' And when Barrett shook his head, Morrissey said, 'No, I thought not,' and dumped the eight files on the sergeant's desk. He took back the Pallister folder. 'Have a look through the rest and tell me if anything strikes you. I'm going to have a word with Beckett.'

He half smiled as he went out. Barrett speechless was a new phenomenon, and one he could quite get to like in time—except that he knew it wouldn't last long.

When Beckett saw the file he grimaced. 'Found my sore spot then? I didn't like this, it had a funny feel all the way along. Nothing I could put my finger on.' He squinted sideways. 'Sounds like one of your sodding hunches, doesn't it, except I don't get 'em, thank God.' He hesitated. 'Fact is, I was looking for a body. Didn't find one but that's what I was looking for.'

'No doubts?'

Beckett shook his head. 'One of them where you know what the bloody answer is and can't prove a damn thing. We got the dogs out, borrowed men from all over the place and found sod-all. Nice family too,' he said thoughtfully. 'Had to go through the routine but I don't think either of them had a hand in it; bloody good actors if they had.'

'Nothing else in your head that isn't in the file?'

'Nothing. Want to take it off my hands then?'

'If you don't object.'

'Be my guest. Just don't make me look a complete latherhead. Linking it up?'

'Let's say I've had my attention drawn to a lot of coincidences. I want to make certain they're really there and not just illusion.'

'Good luck.' Beckett neatened the file and handed it back. 'If you find anything...'

Morrissey nodded and went back to his office. Barrett looked up.

'Too many,' he said.

Morrissey gave him the Pallister folder.

'Find out how many the NSPCC have on file...'

'Right.'

'And then do the same with Social Services.'

Barrett grimaced.

'Go bang my head on a brick wall, you mean.' He saw the morning disappearing down a series of endless corridors as he was passed from one office to another. In theory, inter-disciplinary co-operation was fine, in practice it was laughable. 'Do I take these with me?' he waved at the files.

'Don't be daft,' Morrissey said. 'We want to look at their files, not show them ours.'

TWENTY-TWO

THE CORONATION ESTATE had earned a rough reputation. Malminster had three council estates, none of them high-rise. Two were largely respectable, but the third had collected more than its fair share of trouble-makers and problem families. If asked, the housing department always denied any direct policy of lumping them all together in one place, but the fact was no one else would accept a house up there.

Philip Duffin had lived on Queen Elizabeth Crescent; a semi-circle of houses with scrubby patches that were supposed to be gardens. The Duffin house had lost its fence, but had knee-high grass and a broken pram in its place. No doubt if the grass were cut there would be other, even less enticing debris beneath.

Morrissey got out of his car; was it imagination that gave everything a greyish hue? Pavement, path, cement facing, even the grass itself held a greyish tinge of decay, and the dull, overcast sky laid on an extra depth of depression.

As he stood outside the door the chief inspector could see a green glass vase in the window holding red, orange and violet plastic flowers. Inside, a child wailed desolately. He knocked heavily and the sound increased. He expected the door to be locked but when he tried the handle it swung open onto a narrow hall, and a sad brown carpet subdued by grime. Through the open door of the kitchen he could see pots and pans stacked in the sink. The crying came from upstairs and there was no other sound in the house.

He stood on the bottom step and called out. The wailing stopped, but after a few seconds began again. Morrissey went upstairs.

The child was harnessed into a wooden cot that stank damply; a little girl about two years old in an out-grown sleeping suit that was stained and wet. Saliva dripped from her bottom lip. There was no other furniture in the room, just bare floorboards and a greyish soft toy. He picked it up and the child reached out.

Was this how Philip Duffin had lived?

He put the toy in the cot and went to his car radio to ask grimly for a WPC and a social worker. 'Try to get them here in five minutes. Five, not ten,' he repeated, 'is that clear?'

'Yes, sir.'

He slammed the car door and a woman leaned from the bedroom window of the adjoining house and shouted at him. 'What you up to then? She's not in, so you keep out of there.' She was still in her nightdress.

'Did you know there was a child in the house? Where's the mother?'

'She's working, isn't she? What you expect her to do with the bleeding kid, strap it to her back? I'll go and give it a drink in a bit.'

'That's what you usually do is it?' He turned away from her.

'Here, wait on, I'm coming down. You can't go in there on your own. It's not right.'

But it was right to leave a child soiled, wet and miserable.

Morrissey went back up the stairs, squatting at the side of the cot, dancing the grubby rabbit along the rail, talking softly. The wails turned into sobs and the woman came in.

Her yellow hair hadn't been combed and she smelled of unmade beds, but the way the thin cotton wrap was tied around her reminded him of Marion Walsh.

He stood up, and she shifted from one foot to the other.

'You're fuzz,' she said. 'What's Linda been up to?' Her eyes appraised him openly and appreciatively. 'You're a big 'un, aren't you?'

Morrissey ignored her. 'Where's the mother?'

'I told you, working. She comes back at dinner time and feeds the kid. It's only two days a week, and I listen out for her.'

'Where's the father?'

'God knows.'

'He's left?'

'Left? He wasn't never here.' She weighed him up. 'I bet you're after that sod Duffin. Them what was here before Linda. Broke up after that business about the kid. She went to stay at her mother's and I don't know where he went.' She eyed him again. 'Is that who you're after?'

He heard a car stop outside the house and looked at his watch. Eight minutes; he must have achieved a record.

'I want to talk to them.'

'I can only give you her address; he's probably knocking some other poor bitch about now.' She turned and saw the WPC coming up the stairs and the stocky social worker behind her. 'Oh, God!' she said, 'you're going to take her away. Linda'll bloody kill me. Look, I'll take her next door, she'll be all right there.' She moved to the cot and started to fiddle with the straps.

'Leave it,' Morrissey commanded sharply. 'It's too late for that.'

THE CHIEF INSPECTOR was glad to drive away from Queen Elizabeth Crescent, and glad the child had been moved. The WPC had taken one look and bundled the little girl up in a blanket from the mother's bed. The social worker hadn't got a look in, and that had made Morrissey smile. The next step would be a Place of Safety Order, and after that the police would bring charges of neglect, he was coldly determined on it.

Having seen where Mrs Duffin had once lived, Morrissey half expected her mother's home to be a carbon copy, but instead it surprised him by its neat respectability. It was a council house like the other, but on Westmoor, an estate smaller, older, infinitely less hazardous. The gate was firmly on its hinges, the garden well tended.

He wondered belatedly if the woman he had come to see would be at work, but it was she who answered the door to him, bony and tired looking. There was a child of about six clinging to her cotton dress; his face looked spotty and Morrissey eyed him warily. She neither introduced herself nor waited for him to give his name. Instead she said with a hopeless resignation, 'It's Phil, isn't it? You've come about Phil. I knew you would one day.' She held the door wide. 'You'd better come in. I'll just put Billy in his bedroom for a bit and tell Mum. I'd rather you…she…I want her to be there,' she finished dully.

She thought they'd found her son dead, that much was obvious. Was it fair for him not to put that right now? He cleared his throat. 'Mrs Duffin…'

'In a minute,' she gave the boy a small push. 'Upstairs Billy, play with something for a bit. It won't be long. Go on…' another push. 'Don't argue.' The boy sniffed. 'And don't snivel neither or I'll not get you an ice-cream when the van comes.'

Why did threats always seem to work better than promises? Morrissey wondered. 'Mrs Duffin…'

'I'll just get me mum. You go in here. It'll be all right.' In here was the room on his left, the 'best' room, he supposed. The Sunday room where even Billy behaved. Its first impression was overwhelmingly of brass; small, large, hanging, standing, all gleaming like tributes to the Sun god. He didn't sit down.

The mother was an older version of the daughter, but surprisingly less wearied. 'She'll be all right now, our Carol,' she said. 'Where was he then?'

'We haven't found Philip,' Morrissey said, and looked at Carol Duffin. 'I'm sorry, Mrs Duffin, I'm afraid you jumped to the wrong conclusion. My name is Chief Inspector Morrissey, CID, and I'm looking more closely into your son's disappearance. I hoped you wouldn't mind talking to me about it.'

Was it relief or disappointment they showed?

'But I've said it all, it's written down somewhere,' Carol Duffin said. 'I don't know nothing else. I thought you'd come to tell me... I just want it to be over,' she said quite tonelessly, 'and Philip where he ought to be.'

Morrissey was gentle. 'If you could just tell me once more, everything that happened around the time Philip went,' he coaxed, 'we won't bother you again.'

'Nothing happened. He just went,' she said, 'he didn't tell me or nothing. He'd stayed away before but only when there'd been trouble between him and his dad, and I'd known about it then. He always went somewhere safe. But that day he went to school, and

then he went to choir practice and he never come
home.'

'And there had been no trouble between him and
your husband at that time?'

'No. Well there couldn't have been; he drove the
lorries, and he'd gone up to Scotland. There was only
me and Billy. Phil liked Billy; looked after him real
good for me.' She folded her arms across her waist,
hugging herself.

Perhaps that was the only comfort she'd known
until she came back here, he thought. He said, 'And
there'd been no change in behaviour? Philip hadn't
more money than he should have had, perhaps? Even
a small thing that might seem unimportant to you
could help us to find out what happened. *Anything*,'
he repeated.

The two women exchanged glances. 'Tell him,' the
mother urged. 'Can't hurt Philip now.' She looked at
Morrissey. 'He'd been giving his mum bits of money;
that no-good father of his never gave her enough.'

'Is that right?' Morrissey said, looking at Mrs
Duffin.

She nodded, her head down. 'I didn't like taking it,
I thought he might have been pinching it from school.
But nobody said anything about things going missing. I don't know where he got it. He wouldn't tell
me. It wasn't much, a couple of pounds every week
or so for about two months.'

'And how did he seem when he gave it to you?' the chief inspector asked. 'Pleased, embarrassed, guilty...?'

'None of them,' she said. 'He was just a lot quieter for a bit.'

TWENTY-THREE

'A LOT QUIETER for a bit.' The words stayed in Morrissey's head as he drove away. They brought with them a quickening of nervous activity, a sense that if he only knew where the money had come from he would have the answer to what had happened. Sometimes hunches were a curse.

When he was clear of the estate he pulled into the side of the road and checked the file; the money hadn't been mentioned before.

It was easy to guess why. When it still looked as if Philip might return home his mother had stayed silent, half afraid he might be stealing, but now... Now it seemed she instinctively knew her son would never come home—that had been obvious in every glance, every movement—and so she had disclosed that one thing more. The question was: would it help?

He turned left through a maze of side streets, to come out almost opposite the back entrance of Fisher Comprehensive. Because of Mike, he already knew and respected its common-sense headmaster, and he expected that would be a help. There was nothing pedantic about George Gresham: he wouldn't try to hide anything behind a smokescreen of regulations.

He walked up the steps to the main school building, a fine example of Victorian Gothic, its pillars and
gargoyles still intact. Until the surge for egalitarian-
ism swept it away, Fisher Comp had been St John
Fisher Grammar School, and Morrissey vaguely regretted its passing.

Treading the main hall, its ceiling arched and high,
he debated how many school records were kept on
paper and how many simply remained inside the
heads of individual teachers, to be preserved or forgotten according to the memorability of child or
event.

'I thought the whole thing had died a death,' said
Gresham, when he knew what Morrissey wanted. 'We
had a police officer round twice, uniformed, when it
first happened. He seemed satisfied it was the usual
kind of runaway.' His fingers played idly with a biro,
turning it over on the blotter, end to end. Finally he
snapped it down with an angry movement. 'It's bad
and it's frustrating to get a lad like Duffin and find
he's got a brain, because the Duffins of this world are
better off without one. Your own boy, for example,
is no doubt encouraged, praised, and knows you
provide a safety net; that's the way all families would
be in an ideal world. Duffin would be more likely to
earn a clip for being clever.'

'His parents have split up. I haven't found the father yet. Was he the type to cause trouble at school or
did he keep it inside the home?'

'He raised merry hell a couple of times when we asked him to pay for things his son needed; tight-fisted bastard wouldn't provide anything. No sports gear, no school outings.' Gresham was glowering and Morrissey had the impression that it was less from what he had just said than from what he hadn't said.

Yet a school this size would have parents who found it hard to provide extras, and he didn't believe the headmaster was anything but a fair man. The clear implication was that Duffin could have paid up with ease if he hadn't been bloody-minded.

'In other words Duffin wasn't hard up, he just kept his money for other things,' he hazarded.

'He's the type of man who brags about being able to put away ten to fifteen pints a night,' Gresham said with some bitterness.

And in between times he drove an articulated lorry, Morrissey thought, picturing the lethal combination. Easy now to see why Philip's mother had been grateful for the little bit of money her son had begun to take home. He asked, 'Was there much pilfering going on around the time the boy disappeared; any regular small amounts of money?'

'There's always pilfering going on as I'm sure you know from Mike. I don't recall it being any worse at that time. What do you call small amounts? Fifty pence maybe?'

'Two or three pounds every week.'

'That I would have remembered. No, Chief Inspector, nothing like that. Can I ask what made you bring it up?'

'He'd begun giving that amount to his mother; she was kept short too.'

Gresham winced. 'Is it important?'

'It could be,' Morrissey acknowledged. 'The money had to come from somewhere. There's another Fisher pupil I need to ask about too, a Jason Wood. According to our records he left home six months prior to the Duffin boy.'

'Yes. Quite a lad, our Jason. I seem to remember we always had singular difficulty finding him at all,' said Gresham. 'Habitual truanting. His parents were either due in court or had just been there for failure to ensure school attendance. They were a weak couple, not blessed with much intelligence and Jason was a wild one; I don't think the summons would have done much good. To be honest it didn't surprise me when he went. I'd advise a word with education welfare, they could tell you a lot about Jason. I believe his file was quite bulky.'

'So you weren't surprised about Jason but you were about Philip?'

'Yes,' Gresham said carefully. 'Philip was a different boy altogether.'

'Were they friendly enough to have talked about the idea of leaving home, planned to meet up somewhere?'

'Jason and Philip? Highly unlikely. Jason was the kind of lad Philip kept away from. Too many fists flying at home probably to cope with the same sort of thing at school.'

'Jason was the school bully?'

'Not exactly.' Gresham was being careful again. 'More that some people seem to be born as victims and Philip was in that category. Life is never fair, is it?'

'Hardly ever,' Morrissey agreed. 'Thanks, I have a clear picture now.'

He got up to go and Gresham went with him to the door. 'Why are questions being asked again after all this time?' he asked bluntly. 'Something new must have come up for a chief inspector to involve himself.'

'Someone roused my curiosity and at the moment that's really all there is to it.' Morrissey held out his hand and added, 'If anything comes out of it, I'll let you know.'

Through the plain glass pane in 5B's classroom door Mike saw him go, and his mind slid away from the problem in physics he was supposed to be concentrating on. Philip Duffin had been all right really and he felt guilty he hadn't had the courage to say so at the time. There was something else he had never said too, something his father would want to know. He knew where Philip had gone after choir practice that night. With a hand in his pocket he eased the wrapper from a toffee and contemplated the difficulties of divided loyalty.

BARRETT COUNTED the morning a success; he had encountered no walls of resistance, no reluctance to delve into files. He guessed the unusual air of co-operation stemmed more from desperation at having lost contact with four children than from a new sense of friendliness for policemen, but the reason didn't matter; only the end result counted—and the end result this time was a lot of useful information. Some of it, he was certain, wouldn't have been passed on before. The only blank had been Ian Pallister.

He was whistling when he reached the office, cheerful, the previous night's worries behind him. The chief inspector wasn't back, and the canteen was open. He went in search of a chip butty and left the papers on his desk. Morrissey saw them there when he came in a few minutes later and took them to his own desk to read. He was doing that when the telephone rang.

The call was totally unexpected and no longer his concern. He listened and stared at the papers on his desk, seeing the psychiatrist's intense face in his mind's eye. Mrs Cotton was starting to remember things, and some of the images she was bringing up were disturbingly consistent. Did he want to call in at the unit?

What the devil did "disturbingly consistent" mean? 'The case has been closed,' said Morrissey heavily.

'Yes, I guessed that,' Reynolds returned, 'but I thought personal interest, perhaps?'

Morrissey stabbed a pencil at the blotter and saw the point snap. Personal interest; there was certainly that.

'Any particular time?'

'I'll be available between three and four if you happen to be passing.'

'I probably will,' said Morrissey. 'Thanks.'

'Don't mention it. Even a psychiatrist like myself has need to have his curiosity eased occasionally,' Reynolds said with an odd little laugh.

TWENTY-FOUR

BARRETT HAD EXPECTED to spend the afternoon with Morrissey but instead he was on his own. The chief inspector had left him to organise a trace on Les Duffin, and that was already under way. He had also handed him the files for two of the missing boys: the first, Paul White, had left home in January last year; the second, Stephen Howarth, and the most recently missing, had been gone four months.

It was a sign of the detective sergeant's state of mind that he accepted working alone as a sign of grace; his sins had been forgiven and his abilities recognised. In that mood he drove onto the Coronation Estate, thinking that passing his next promotion exams would be a breeze, and that Inspector Barrett had a good ring to it.

The truth was quite different. For the time being he was out of favour.

Morrissey would be the first to admit Barrett's potential, but the cocky dismissiveness he had shown in the Walsh case still rankled, and his off-duty adventures were a source of irritation. The chief inspector was keeping him out of sight and occupied. Eventually there would be rehabilitation, but it would be in Morrissey's own good time.

In the meantime Morrissey pursued his own line.
The headmaster of Fisher's had been correct about
the size of the file education welfare had held on Jason Wood. Rescued from the basement, it gaped and
bulged. All that, Morrissey marvelled, for a lad barely
thirteen.

Anne Daley, who had dealt with Jason and his
problems, was brisk and quite unsentimental. 'The
one certain thing about Jason,' she said, 'was that
he'd end up in trouble with your lot. It was only a
matter of time. His parents had no control over him
at all, he ran rings round them.'

'But he hadn't actually been in juvenile court,'
Morrissey said, 'or we'd have had records too.'

She smiled. 'You never caught him at it, and it's
not for me to tell. I'm only supposed to get him to
school and make sure he's fed, clothed and out of
danger.'

'And was he?' asked Morrissey. 'All of those?'

She looked at him obliquely. 'He was fed and
clothed. As far as the danger bit goes—well, we don't
know where he is, do we?'

'No. If we did the problem would still be yours and
not mine.'

'*Touché*, Chief Inspector.' She smiled and opened
the folder tie. 'Jason started truanting at eight and it's
kept on growing. His biggest problem was having
those particular parents. They're not mentally sub-
normal, not officially anyway, but they must be borderline. They have five other children, all younger

than Jason, and only the youngest shows signs of being anything but dull, thank God.'

She caught Morrissey's raised eyebrows and grimaced. 'Sounds terrible, doesn't it, but imagine five more files this size. The youngest starts school next year; but by the time he's old enough for Fisher's, I intend to be gone.'

Morrissey could sympathise in principle; there were a few faces he would rather not see around Malminster. 'Not a case of child abuse, then?'

'God, no; if he hadn't gone off it would have been the other way round before long. Have you met his mother and father?'

'Not yet,' Morrissey admitted.

'Well, go easy. I've had to take them to court three times and it's given me the grandmother of a guilt complex. I mean, what can they do? The father's only five feet four; another year and Jason would have passed him.' She rubbed her russet-grey hair, stirring it into life.

Ten, fifteen years ago, Morrissey thought, she would have turned heads. He wondered why she had chosen education welfare, and as if she caught his thought she said, 'It's a thankless job; maybe we're all masochists. The lame looking after the lame.' She gave Morrissey another sideways glance. 'I heard it said once that when the percentage of crimes solved goes up, it's because there are more crooks on your side than theirs.'

Morrissey laughed. 'I'll remember that,' he promised, 'for when the Chief Super starts getting cocky.'

She grinned and he knew they had passed a barrier. 'Jason did a nice little line in shop-lifting,' she confided. 'Sweets, lighters, pens, cigarettes; things he could sell easily for pocket money.'

'And what did he do with the pocket money?' Morrissey asked.

'Bought himself more sweets, went to the pictures, hung around with older boys. He didn't get into glue sniffing, thank God. In fact he told me once it was bloody stupid; his words. Not long before he went walkabout actually.'

Morrissey said quickly, 'Had he been hanging around sniffers?'

'Ye-es, he'd been selling glue.' She went red. 'That makes me sound irresponsible, but I don't believe he would have done it again. I had a soft spot for him,' she said as he looked at her, 'I know that, and I wish I knew what had happened to him.'

'When was the last time you saw him?' the chief inspector said. 'I know it's a long time ago but...'

'It's on the records,' she said, 'even if it wasn't still in my mind.' She turned to the end of the file and looked at the last entry. 'June the eighteenth. I'd been to see his parents and he was walking down the lane.'

'He didn't try to avoid you then?'

'No. We had a sort of understanding. I remember thinking he was growing up. He said he'd had his

photograph taken and been paid two pounds. He
showed me the money.'

'Two pounds,' said Morrissey. 'For a photograph.
Didn't you think it was a bit odd?'

'Yes, but I didn't think he was lying about it.' She
looked at him and saw a knowledge in his eyes that
she hadn't previously entertained. 'Oh God, no,' she
said, clutching at her head. 'A perve with a camera!'

'I hope not,' said Morrissey, 'but I'm trying to
think who else would pay him two pounds.'

MORRISSEY DROVE from the Education Department
to the small, private estate where Ian Pallister's parents still lived. The gardens of the semi-detached
dormer-bungalow were well tended, the paintwork
fresh; a greater contrast between that and the Coronation Estate where Philip Duffin had lived would be
hard to find. But there was a look in Mrs Pallister's
eyes when she opened the door to him that he had
seen before in Carol Duffin's. A first, quick hope,
and then resignation.

'My husband isn't here,' she said. 'But if I can help
you then obviously I will. Come through into the sitting-room.' She closed the door and went before him
down the short hall. 'I thought there might be news,
but I can see from your face there isn't.'

'I'm sorry,' he said, knowing that although he
meant them the words were comfortless. He stood
awkwardly, a tall man in a small room, conscious
more of its emptiness than of himself, sensing that the

house, like the woman, was waiting, and there was nothing he could say to make the emptiness less.

Then a clock in another room chimed twice and she said calmly, 'Can I make you a cup of coffee, or tea perhaps?' And he marvelled at the strength of spirit that let her do that.

'It's kind, but no, I won't stay long,' he said. 'I wanted to ask if Ian had shown any change in behaviour before he went missing.'

'He was quite the same as always, cheerful, helpful. We always encouraged him to bring problems home; had there been any, I'm sure he would have done so.'

'No one had approached him, or frightened him in any way that you know of?'

'No, I'm sorry. Everything seemed quite normal. He came home from school and began his homework while I made his tea, then he changed into his uniform and left the house at quarter past six to go to the scout hut.'

'Is there anyone he might have met and felt it safe to be with; someone with a car perhaps?'

'Only family,' she said protestingly. 'I said that before. He was a very sensible boy. Normally he walked home with Richard, but that day Richard was at home with a cold. If he hadn't been . . .' She forced a smile. 'There now, there's no point in might have beens, is there?'

'If you do think of anything, you or your husband, however insignificant, please give me a call.' He gave her his official card and, as she looked at it, asked casually, 'Do you know anyone who has an interest in photography?'

'Well yes, my husband has, he's been a member of the Malminster club for years.' She looked up. 'Why? Is it important?'

'I shouldn't think so,' said Morrissey, but added it to a growing list of possibilities.

MORRISSEY'S MIND had been trying to follow a tenuous link as he drove from the Pallister home to the psychiatric unit. The link went from the two pounds Philip Duffin had begun giving to his mother weekly, to the two pounds Jason had been paid for a photograph, and from there to Ian Pallister's father and his interest in photography. And then there was the photography club.

As he parked in the visitors' car-park his mind flicked to Robert Goddard. Had he too been a member of the Malminster club?

A perve with a camera had been Anne Daley's words.

Morrissey walked down the long hospital corridor, his feet echoing before him from the tiled walls, and wondered why the psychiatric wings were always last to be modernised.

Reynolds' clinic had just ended, and he looked tired and more than a little depressed, Morrissey thought, as they shook hands. He supposed it went with the territory. Keeping an even keel mentally must be difficult when the whole day was spent among small insanities.

'I'm glad you could come,' Reynolds said. 'I read about the suicide of course. Useful little phrase—the police are not looking for anyone else in connection with their enquiries—not quite an accusation of murder, but near enough.'

'Jargon; you have it too,' Morrissey said.

'A useful cover for lack of knowledge usually. Don't you find that?'

'Or hiding it,' Morrissey said.

'Yes. I think we might both gain something today, Chief Inspector. Shall we look in on Mrs Cotton, then I'll let you see the images she's throwing up?'

See the images, thought Morrissey. Not verbal then.

Marjorie Cotton was in a small, cream-walled room by herself, sitting on a chair that faced the window and looked across a patch of grass and a marching line of conifers. Behind the evergreens Morrissey recognised the single-storey building that housed the mortuary. There were no windows on this side, and it was impossible for Mrs Cotton to know what she was looking at. For some obscure reason Morrissey felt glad.

Reynolds walked around the chair. 'There's a visitor for you, Marjorie,' he said. 'Are you going to say hello to him?' He half tilted the chair and turned it so that she was facing into the room. She looked even smaller than when Morrissey had first seen her, as though the flesh were leaving her bones in protest at things seen. Her eyes blinked but seemed not to focus on anything.

This was ridiculous, the chief inspector thought, and disappointment edged into his mind. Wherever this woman's mind was, it wasn't in the room with them.

She said, without much hope, 'Are you my father?' and Morrissey was half tempted to take her hand and agree that he was to ease the darkness.

Then Reynolds said, 'Not your father, Marjorie, just a friend,' and he realised she had probably asked the same question many times before.

Her head made a small movement that could have meant anything. Morrissey said, 'Hello, Mrs Cotton, I just came by to see if you were feeling better.'

She blinked and said politely, 'Mrs Cotton isn't here today. Would you like to leave a message?'

'Another time,' Morrissey replied. 'Perhaps another time.'

He watched Reynolds turn the chair to the window again and felt anger over-ride disappointment. Coming here had been a complete waste of time. He strode out of the room and waited in the corridor, glowering.

Barrett would have been wary of the look; Reynolds ignored it as he admitted, 'Not very lucid at the moment; it comes and goes. Shall we go to the therapy room and have a look at the images she's throwing up? I was hoping you might tell me if they have any relevance. I gather she was pretty bloody when she was brought in, but of course the case is closed, isn't it?'

'It's closed,' agreed Morrissey, and didn't expand on it.

There were half a dozen patients in the therapy room, working with clay or painting.

Reynolds said, 'This is the most useful way we have of learning what is in a patient's mind. They externalise suppressed images, and some of those images can be quite frightening. You may find these paintings of Mrs Cotton's fall into that category.'

Morrissey looked at the bright, clumsy splashes of paint. Untrained, struggling. Perhaps it was the first time she had tried. Yet his mind recognised and accepted the childish painting of a body, grotesquely crimson. A stick woman at its side, crimson splashed, and beyond the distorted room and a too large door, a blackness that had shape.

'As you see each painting has the same content,' the psychiatrist said calmly. 'Would you say it was an approximation of the murder scene?'

Morrissey would, and was now certain that Marjorie Cotton had seen it too; that much was very plain. Her fingerprints had been on the bottle. But it was Robert Goddard who had killed himself and, officially, Marion Walsh and Betty Hartley.

'It's an accurate representation,' the chief inspector said grudgingly. He moved the painting around. 'This is all she does, nothing else?'

'This is the block her mind refuses to relinquish,' Reynolds said. 'The blackness beyond the door is a deeper block still. I hoped you might have some ideas?'

'No.' Morrissey looked at the arched darkness and felt vague recollection stir.

'It has a shape as you can see, almost like folded wings. Her mind has twisted whatever she saw into a type of primitive image, and somehow I have to get past it to return her to sanity.' He looked at Morrissey. 'I hope I haven't wasted your time.'

'No, you haven't done that,' said the chief inspector. 'You've just given me something else to worry about.'

TWENTY-FIVE

HALF WAY ALONG Stye Lane, Jason Wood's family lived in a run down cottage, a tied dwelling that went with the job of pigman at Brooks' Farm. The rest of the children were already home from school and the kitchen door stood wide open, letting out a squabble of voices and noise. As he laid his knuckles against it Morrissey saw disorder inside. Four children and two cats in a room barely ten feet square; no—five children. The smallest was wedged into a high chair that it had almost outgrown, and whimpered monotonously to be let down into the confusion below.

A Jack Russell showed its teeth from under a sagging sideboard and Morrissey eyed it mistrustfully.

On the hearthrug a man whom the chief inspector supposed must be Wood, cleaned boots, jabbing at caked mud with a bent screwdriver. Morrissey took a step inside and brought out his warrant card; for all the notice that was taken he might be invisible. Clearly, above the noise, he stated his name. At the sink Wood's wife peeled potatoes and gave no sign she had heard, but the man asked with total disinterest, 'Is wanting me?'

'Are you Thomas Wood?'

'Is one of 'em been up to something?'

'No,' Morrissey said. 'I've come to talk about Jason. Away from the children if possible.' The name worked a miracle; the children were silent, staring at him.

Wood's face registered nothing. 'You heard what t'policeman said. Get outside and play in t'garden. Go on or he'll lock you up.'

Morrissey wasn't happy to be used as a threat, it always dismayed him that the policeman had replaced the bogey-man in many homes, but he had the feeling that in this case Wood's authority would have been useless without it.

As it was the children showed signs of standing their ground. Anne Daley's assessment seemed to have been correct.

Wordlessly the woman turned from the sink and lifted the youngest from its chair; this one showed no reluctance to be gone but made a bee-line for the door.

When the last child was out of earshot, Morrissey came straight to the question he had come to ask, instinctively knowing preliminaries would be a waste of time. He asked bluntly, 'Did Jason ever come home and say anything to you about having his photograph taken, or mention anybody with a camera?'

He thought the question he asked was simple enough until Wood answered. 'Had it took when he was a babe. That year we was at Lowestoft. Moll, can you get that photo?' His wife laid aside the potato knife, wiping her hands on the sides of her apron.

'No,' Morrissey said sharply. 'That isn't what I wanted, I'm talking about just before he left home. Did Jason say anything about being paid to have his photograph taken.'

'No, said nothing about that. Come home from school saying he could have it took for a pound, but he never did.'

'Did he act any differently that last week or so, quieter perhaps?' Would either parent have noticed if he had? he thought.

Wood poked dispiritedly at a lump of mud and with something akin to despair Morrissey recognised the futility of trying to stir memories. At the beginning Jason had been missing a fortnight before Wood had reported it; and then it had been a visit by Anne Daley that had spurred him on.

Under the brown farm overall he still wore, the pigman's thin shoulders shrugged. He complained resentfully, 'Can't say anything about quieter, never listen to 'em, less I have to. Too much frigging noise. Well, you heard 'em, didn't you? You heard 'em when you come.'

'Yes, I heard them,' the chief inspector said heavily. 'If you do remember anything...'

'Don't expect we shall.' Wood went back to his boots, and Morrissey gave up and returned to his car; two of Wood's children sat on the bonnet, their heels drumming hard against the metal. They giggled when he set them down.

BARRETT HAD UNEARTHED nothing new and it rankled. Everything he had asked had brought only
monosyllables or abuse, and he simmered with pent-
up frustration. Belatedly he asked himself if Morrissey had guessed it would be a time-wasting afternoon. And then he had to cool his heels at the office
and wait for the chief to return. When he did he told
his sad tale.

Morrissey listened without sympathy. 'At least
when you go back you'll know what to expect,' he
said, studiously not seeing Barrett's discontent. 'We
need to know if either boy talked about being approached by anyone, stranger or not, to have his
photograph taken, that's one thing; the other is if they
had any more money than usual—you'd better ask
around their friends and school as well.'

'Something's come up?' There was expectancy in
the question.

Morrissey eyed him; something had, but he wasn't
disposed to share what were only tenuous feelings. He
told Barrett the barest fact. 'The Wood boy was approached and told his welfare officer.'

'That's all?'

'It's something,' Morrissey returned, gathering the
files together. 'Let's make it an early night, shall we?'

He was home before seven and Margaret greeted
him warmly. 'Thanks,' she said. 'The grapevine's
been busy, you've been stirring things up.'

He grunted. 'That's good?'

'That's good.' She picked up the meat mallet and pounded at a piece of steak. 'I suppose you can't talk about it?'

'I can tell you three out of the eight turned up again. The grapevine slipped up there.'

She said cheerfully, 'It did, didn't it? Which three?' When he told her she nodded. 'Madge Willis gave us those; she's stopped teaching now, so she wouldn't have heard. I'm glad they're back. What about the others?'

He shook his head. 'I'm worried,' he said, and went upstairs.

Soon after they moved into the house Morrissey had made the boxroom into a study for himself; there wasn't enough room to swing a proverbial cat but it was somewhere he could work in peace when he needed to. He was there when his son came to find him and tell him dinner was ready, working on an old pine table that served as a desk. Nosey as usual, Mike leaned on his father's shoulder and read the name on the open file.

'Ian Pallister. Who's he then?'

'A boy who went missing like Phil Duffin.'

'Oh yeah, it was in the local paper. You were away and Mum wouldn't let me go out.' Aggrievement for the past injustice lurked in his voice. 'Not found him either?'

'No.' Morrissey closed the file. 'And I've told you before about reading over my shoulder.'

Mike ignored the rebuke and grinned. 'That's why you had it,' he said. 'It was Pallister's.'

The chief inspector frowned at his son. 'What was?'

'Oh come on, Dad! The woggle of course. IP—Ian Pallister; and I suppose the 7 meant Seventh Scouts.'

'Tell your mother I'll be down in a minute,' Morrissey said and opened his briefcase. He thought: from the mouths of babes and sucklings...

He listened to Mike's feet running downstairs.

Instinct had insisted the Walsh case hadn't ended; now, without knowing it, his son had given him something to use as a lever to open it up again.

Everything had pointed to the Little Henge murders revolving around petty blackmail; but supposing that was only a part of it, the way it had cleverly been made to look.

Marion Walsh could have been playing a larger, more dangerous fish.

The phrase "a cool psychopath" came back to him again, niggling as it had since Jim Reed first uttered it.

Someone with more to lose than a coffee-cup reputation. *Not* Robert Goddard.

TWENTY-SIX

MORRISSEY WAS UP EARLY.

'But you *need* a hot breakfast,' Margaret scolded. 'You know darned well how often you miss lunch.'

Morrissey, gulping coffee, shook his head. 'I won't starve,' he promised, wincing as he felt rather than heard the faint rip of sleeve lining. It crossed his mind that his suit might need replacing; Margaret had been nagging him to do that for months. No. That wasn't fair. Margaret was one of the few wives who didn't nag. What then? Persistently suggested. He smiled, feeling a stir of affection, and kissed her with a suddenly embarrassed clumsiness. Michael came into the kitchen barefoot and in pyjama bottoms, still blinking with sleep.

'Dad...'

'Not now, Mike, it'll have to keep,' he said, then guilt added, 'Not something that won't, is it?'

'I don't suppose so.' Mike wasn't sure though as he watched his father pick up his briefcase and leave. The truth was, conscience or something very like it had been worrying at him since he had seen his father at school yesterday. Only then had he thought seriously that anything terrible might have happened to Duffin; before it had just been a bit of a breeze.

Didn't everyone fantasise about leaving home, even if home was stable and happy, and Duffin's he knew with a hundred per cent certainty hadn't been that.

Morrissey, knowing nothing of what was in his son's mind, put him out of his own, concentrating it instead on what he expected to be a difficult interview. This morning he had to tell the chief superintendent he would be opening up the Little Henge business again, and Osgodby would not be pleased. But, pleased or not, it would be difficult to dismiss the fact that an item of scout uniform, probably belonging to a missing boy, had been found at The Beeches.

As he negotiated the roundabout Morrissey wondered what time Ian Pallister's father left for work. What he needed now was a positive identification of the leather ring, because if he had that he also had undeniable grounds for digging deeper.

And for suggesting to Osgodby that Goddard's death was not suicide, but a third, meticulously brutal murder.

It took a little time to retrieve the woggle from the bowels of a system that hated to go into reverse, and when he got back to his car the morning traffic was already heavy. A surge of acid reached his empty stomach and he winced at the warning stab of pain. He wanted both Pallisters to be there this time. Not just to identify evidence, but so that he could get a look at the father.

A grey Sierra was just beginning to reverse in the bungalow drive. The chief inspector stopped his own car halfway across the opening and got out, hearing an impatient blast of horn.

He showed his warrant. 'I'd like to talk about Ian, Mr Pallister.' All anger drained from the man's face and the Sierra's engine stilled.

When he emerged from the car Donald Pallister was thin, but it was a thinness that looked as if weight had dropped from him. Morrissey looked at the shadowed eyes behind steel-rimmed spectacles and knew that this father at least mourned his son.

'There's news?'

Morrissey shook his head.

'No. I have something I should like you to look at and then tell me if you have ever seen before.'

'Something of Ian's?' Pallister's shoulders seemed to sag even more as he turned and walked back down the side path to the kitchen. Mrs Pallister was washing up, but stopped when Morrissey came in, hastily pulling off her rubber gloves. They looked at him expectantly. When he put the woggle on the table Mrs Pallister's face crumpled. 'It's Ian's,' she said. 'Where did you find it?'

'Can you be absolutely sure?'

Pallister reached out a hand.

'He cut his initials into it the day he got it.' His hand was steady as he held it closer to his eyes. 'Yes, it's Ian's. There's no doubt. Can you tell us where you found it?'

'I'm sorry. That isn't something I can tell you.' Morrissey put the woggle into its plastic bag and tucked it into his inside pocket. He could sense the unspoken questions and hoped they wouldn't be asked.

'Sometimes all we want is for the whole thing to be over,' Mrs Pallister said. 'After that...' She shook her head. 'I suppose life must have some purpose though it's hard to see what it might be. Losing a child leaves such an emptiness.' Her eyes were without tears and Morrissey knew instinctively that she had passed that point, that grief had reached a deeper level. And he could say nothing that might relieve it.

When he asked about the photography club, and more specifically if Ian had known any member well enough to have accepted a lift, Donald Pallister looked puzzled.

He said, 'He'd been to a couple of meetings but he wasn't all that interested. He certainly didn't know anyone well. Is there a suggestion...?'

'It's a question no one asked before,' Morrissey said, 'and that's all it is at the moment. Do you know if Robert Goddard was a member?'

'Yes, he'd been with us for five or six years. It was a shock when we...' Pallister broke off and his eyes examined Morrissey's face. 'I won't ask, Chief Inspector,' he said carefully, 'because I know you can't tell me, but I don't think Ian ever met him.'

'What about a man called Wellen? Lennie Wellen?'

'No, that's a name I haven't heard mentioned. I can look it up if you like but I'm sure I would know.'

Mrs Pallister moved closer to her husband, her hand reaching automatically for his. Pallister took it in his own and gripped it tightly. He said hesitantly, 'It's almost over, isn't it?'

'I hope so,' Morrissey replied gently, knowing in his heart that for them, like many parents, it might never end.

THE WALSH FILE was bulky with things read and unread. Barrett, watching Morrissey search through, and for some reason unknown to himself wary, said, 'I thought we'd finished with the Walsh file.'

'Yes, I know you did,' Morrissey was acerbic. 'But if you remember my own thoughts on the matter were different. If anyone asks for me I'll be upstairs with the superintendent.' He eyed Barrett. 'Get some writing up done,' he advised. 'You might find you need it in a hurry.'

As the door closed, a prickle of discomfort edged into Barrett's mind. He told himself there was no way the Old Man would agree to activating the Little Henge business again; like Goddard it was dead as a dodo. The certainty was short-lived and after a couple of minutes he discovered an urge to catch up on his desk work; he reminded himself that, as the saying went, it was better to be a live dog than a dead lion, and the chief had been looking uncomfortably sure of himself again.

Osgodby was suffering from a similar form of misgiving. He wanted to believe the damned woggle had been introduced simply to let the chief inspector back into the Little Henge murders. But the forensic report Morrissey had laid on his desk was dated *before* he had slammed the case closed, and part of a fingerprint belonging to the Walsh woman had been inside the leather ring. And so he smarted and listened to Morrissey's argument, and when it was finished said, 'You're telling me a psychopathic paedophile has been operating in and around Malminster for at least a year and we haven't known about it. Not only that, but to cover up he's killed three people at Little Henge. I'd like to tell you to go away and see an analyst, but I can't do that because you've made it fit so bloody well.' He sucked on his teeth and barked, 'Even if you're right, there's a chance it was all down to Goddard.'

Morrissey wasn't going to be drawn into subjective disquiet. 'I don't think we can take that chance,' he said. 'Do you?'

'No, damn it, but you're a thorn in my side, Morrissey. Do you want to open up the incident room?'

'I don't think it would help this time. I'd like it to look as if we're still satisfied.'

'Do things the way you want, just don't bring any bricks down.' Osgodby leaned forward. 'I hope you're wrong, John, but if you're not, try to close it fast.'

Morrissey thought about Mike standing in the kitchen that morning. With two boys missing from Fisher's, he didn't need to be told about urgency. But Osgodby would know that too. The real crux for the chief superintendent was fear that this new situation would be made public, and Morrissey didn't envy him the inevitable explanation the chief constable would expect.

TWENTY-SEVEN

BARRETT HAD KNOWN from Morrissey's face that the chief inspector had got his own way, and like Chicken Licken had waited for the sky to fall. But Morrissey was in reasonable humour, and apart from reminding Barrett pointedly about the necessity of visiting the Whites and Howarths again, chose not to rub in the fact that the sergeant's self-congratulation over the Walsh case had been ill-judged.

Silently Barrett reflected that both his private and his professional life had taken a distinct downturn. He picked up the files from the chief inspector's desk and quit the office, refusing to let himself speculate how long the run of bad luck might last.

Morrissey came across the name Wellen in a report from the Met that had been filed away unread. The plump art lover from *Cobblers* had been taking the wrong kind of photographs for a long time, and had probably introduced a lot of people, besides Marion Walsh, to the business of pornography, but it was the first link the chief inspector had found between the dead woman's past and her life in Little Henge. And Marion had renewed the acquaintance; the book of matches proved that.

The really interesting question was when and why.

Wellen had denied knowing her. What would he say when faced with proof? Would he plead panic, or a fresh start?

Morrissey wondered how many of the borderline "art" shots in the wine bar's back room were Wellen's work, and remembered the boys he had seen hanging around outside. When he had seen them from his car he had thought they were from Fisher Comp.

Was it Wellen who had promised Jason Wood two pounds to be photographed, and later persuaded Philip Duffin to do the same thing?

Morrissey went downstairs, knowing that the big computer would now get him information in one or two hours about Wellen's past activities that once would have taken days to recover. There was still a faint smell of bacon hanging around in the back corridor and on the way back to his own office Morrissey called in at the canteen and took a pot of coffee and a bacon butty back with him to stem the flow of acid in his stomach.

'I DON'T SEE any other option,' Morrissey said implacably an hour later. 'Goddard wouldn't have stayed passive while cyanide was poured down his throat. We need a second PM to decide things one way or the other.'

'And what about the inquest?' Osgodby snapped. 'I suppose you expect me to cancel that too?'

'In the circumstances, yes.'

'Because in your opinion it wasn't suicide.'

'In my opinion,' Morrissey agreed, 'it wasn't. The first post-mortem didn't cover all possibilities; a second must.'

'You do realise I'm going to have to clear it with the CC, and he's already feeling foul about his brother-in-law. You'd better hope you're right. Who's going to let the widow know?'

'I am.'

As the words were said, Morrissey thought of Helen and felt glad he would see her again. Then he wondered what her reaction would be. Relief that at last there was official doubt? If so, relief would be mixed with guilt because she had accepted the police verdict in the first place, and even now he couldn't tell her with certainty that it had been wrong.

When she opened the door to him he was shocked. Her eyes were darkly dull and lines of tiredness were etched across her face. She didn't attempt to smile but simply said, 'I hadn't expected to see you again,' and held the door wide to let him pass.

Except for her the house was empty. Where were the family who should be there giving her support?

When he asked she shook her head.

'It was entirely my choice. It seemed a much better idea for the children to stay at university where they can put things out of their minds—and I've never been close to Robert's family.'

'But your own?' he insisted.

'There are only my parents and I don't want them to come down from Scotland. It would be too horrendous for them.'

It was horrendous for *her* without anyone, Morrissey thought; or didn't that count?

She took him into the once-friendly sitting-room and sat in one of the chairs. He stood awkwardly, his discomfort unnatural to him. The ticking of the ormolu clock on the mantelshelf seemed too loud.

'I've asked for a second post-mortem,' he told her abruptly. 'I'm not satisfied that your husband's death was suicide.' She stared, frowning until the words sank in fully, and then her face seemed to come alive.

'I didn't think anything could be said about Robert that I wouldn't find unbearable,' she said. 'I've dreaded every knock at the door in case it was some smart reporter from one of the less reputable newspapers, looking for something to write about. The children... Well, you know how they must feel—you have children of your own. As things are they can shut it out, but if it got into the national press... I've been terrified,' she said simply, and got up and came to stand before him, resting her hands lightly on his arms. 'If it wasn't suicide, then Robert didn't do those appalling things. That's what you're really saying, isn't it?'

Morrissey fought down a powerful urge to put his own arms around her, and wondered when she had last had a decent night's sleep; her eyes were almost feverish as she waited for him to answer her.

'If I'm right,' he said gruffly. 'That still has to be proved, though.'

'But you *will* prove it,' she said with a sudden unnatural brightness. 'I'll make some coffee. It's too chilly to sit outside as we did before, but we can drink it in the kitchen and look out at the forsythia. It's starting to drop now; I always wish it would last forever. Do you have forsythia?'

'No,' he said. 'I've sometimes thought about putting one where it will catch the sun, but I haven't done it yet.'

He followed her to the kitchen, not because he wanted coffee, but to prolong the meeting and because he knew she needed it. Watching her pour milk from bottle to jug he remembered Ida Hodge's remark at the cemetery, and wondered if Helen would still remember what time her husband had left on the morning Betty Hartley died.

He asked as they sat at the table, and there was no hesitation in her answer.

'Of course I remember, it would be hard to forget. He left a little before eight, earlier than usual. We'd been on the point of quarrelling, and he was eager to get out.'

'Had the milk been delivered then?'

'I don't think so. No. I remember it was on the back step when I came home from the post office.'

He stared through the window at the bright yellow cascade. It worried him that, without the Pallister link, Goddard's death would have closed all investigation. He wanted the law to be infallible and he didn't like to be reminded that on rare occasions it might not be.

'Robert had a good side to his nature,' Helen said.

Morrissey nodded and told her gently, 'You wouldn't have married him otherwise.'

'No,' she agreed, 'I wouldn't.'

IT WAS ON HIS WAY back to Malminster that Morrissey thought once more about the higher concentration of cyanide in Betty Hartley's cup. Bartholomew had said the dead woman was expecting a friend; someone who could have slipped more poison into her cup while Betty's back was turned.

Someone who drank their coffee black... Like Helen Goddard.

BARRETT CAME BACK TO the office at eleven-thirty, having trodden a lot of old ground without any real benefit. He felt bitter; a DC could have done the job equally well, it didn't take a sergeant to go dogsbodying around, and what made it worse was the knowledge that Morrissey would have been aware of it too. As he climbed the stairs he took time to wonder if the chief were giving him a taste of what demotion would be like.

He wasn't allowed to stay in the office long enough to ask, for as soon as Morrissey saw the negative expression on Barrett's face he said, 'Another wasted morning? Never mind, you can work it out of your system by finding yourself a WPC and getting a statement from the Pallisters. They've identified the woggle that turned up at the Walsh house as belonging to their son; we want it in writing.'

Barrett went red. 'I didn't know that,' he protested. 'How am I supposed to know what's going on if no one tells me?'

'I've just told you,' Morrissey said.

'Smythe's in,' Barrett said sulkily. 'He could go while I got up to date on things.'

'He's not on the case,' Morrissey pointed out. 'You are.' He allowed himself a smile as Barrett stalked out; the sergeant was starting to smart and that was the way it should be.

Soon after twelve the duty sergeant rang to say Mike was asking for him downstairs. Morrissey was surprised. His son didn't normally come to the police station uninvited and he wondered what had brought him this time. His mind went back to early morning and Mike in pyjamas wanting to talk. He realised he had dismissed whatever it was without even giving Mike a hearing; was that why his son had come now? He looked at the mess of papers on his desk and sighed.

'Have him come up,' he told the sergeant. 'And if anyone has time to go to the canteen, two mugs of coffee and two chip butties would be nice.'

He heard a laugh. 'Sounds like conscience payment, sir.'

'Sounds like you know all about such things,' Morrissey riposted as he hung up.

Mike walked up to his father's office slowly. He had known all morning what he was going to do and he half expected to get a ticking off for keeping quiet for so long, but how was he supposed to know when things were so serious? As he climbed the last flight of stairs he saw his father standing on the landing above, looking incredibly official, and for a moment his nerve almost failed.

Then Morrissey said, 'Mike, nice surprise. What have you come to talk about?' and he knew it would be all right.

'I was going to tell you this morning,' Mike said as they went into the chief inspector's office, 'something else about Duffin.' He turned and faced his father seriously. 'I know you told me to tell you everything, but I didn't. I didn't tell you where he was going that night after choir practice,' he said. 'I'm sorry, Dad.'

TWENTY-EIGHT

MORRISSEY KNEW BETTER than to push too hard. The one thing common to all schoolboys was a horror of ratting on one's friends, and it was obvious that Mike felt he was coming very close to that. For that reason the chief inspector waited until they were eating companionably before he began to dig.

But Mike had already decided to tell his father everything.

'I think Duffin probably heard about it from Woodsy. He...'

'You mean Jason Wood?' Morrissey asked.

Mike looked at him uneasily. 'Yes. Woodsy kept on about it being an easy way to make money. He wanted me to go with him once.'

'But you didn't go?' said Morrissey, looking at him quickly.

'We-ell, I didn't fancy it much,' Mike confessed, and Morrissey felt relief. 'He got two pounds for having his photograph taken in this upstairs room. He said he just posed around. He wasn't having me on.' Mike was suddenly on the defensive.

'When was this, just before he stopped coming to school?'

'Couple of weeks before, I think. He was spreading it around that he'd been offered a job in London by this man he met when he was posing once. None of us believed him. He wasn't old enough to get a job anyway.'

Morrissey didn't contradict him. Whatever innocence there was in Mike had to be protected. Or was the naivety assumed for his benefit? It wasn't long since Mike had joked about rent boys. He pushed that problem to the back of his mind. Either way it didn't affect the case, it was strictly a family concern. He asked, 'How did Duffin come into it?'

'Well, he'd heard Woodsy bragging about the money, and he never had anything, not a sausage. So he went down and asked. I don't think he liked it, but he'd have done anything to get his hands on some cash.'

Morrissey sighed. 'Mike, I know you don't want to tell me but I'd like to know who else has been involved. It may be that those boys will be needed to give evidence. You do realise that what you've told me points to some very suspect goings-on.'

Mike looked acutely embarrassed. 'Because *Cobblers* is a gay club, you mean. That makes it worse, doesn't it?'

Morrissey said carefully, 'It might do, depending on all sorts of things. It could be enticement and that's an offence.'

'I'd rather just tell you about Duffin.'

'That's all right, Mike, but give it a bit of thought later.'

Morrissey wanted to ask if any boys from Fisher's went to *Cobblers* for an illicit drink, but thought better of it. There were some things it wouldn't be fair to ask and that was one of them. Instead he asked, 'Is that everything? Nothing else you remember and want to tell me about?'

Mike, who had still eaten only part of his butty, pushed the rest away. He blurted, 'Duffin told me that after choir practice, he was going to go to the club. And there was a punter coming to take special photos, and he was going to get twenty pounds from him.' Mike scowled fiercely, the way he used to when he was small and trying hard not to cry. His father recognised the sign.

'What was he going to do with the money?' he asked quietly.

'He was going to buy football strip,' Mike said.

Morrissey made a mental note to add that to Les Duffin's sin sheet when they found him. Thinking he now knew the cause of his son's distress, he said, 'Thanks, Mike, you've done a very praiseworthy and difficult thing and I appreciate it.' But his son continued to stare at a point on the desk and didn't respond. Something else was bothering him. Morrissey said gently, 'What is it, Mike?'

When the silence grew he let it, knowing his son had to take his time. The answer, when it came, made Morrissey fight down a smile at the opening words, and he was glad Mike hadn't seen it when he heard the rest.

His son said seriously, 'Well, I was younger last year and a lot thicker than I am now.' His eyes moved from the desk to his father's face. 'Do you think it would have made any difference if I'd told you about it then? For Duffin, I mean.' And Morrissey, who had decided a long time ago never to lie to his children in the hope that they would never lie to him, said no and saw Mike's face brighten. He had answered the question and eased his son's burden. What he hadn't said was that it might have made a difference to Ian Pallister, and that was something he hoped Mike would never know.

He walked back downstairs with his son, talking amiably about American football and the possibility of them both getting to see a live game, and Mike was going out of the door when Morrissey asked his final question. 'Did Duffin and Wood go to *Cobblers* on any one particular day?'

'Duffin always went Thursdays, after choir practice, but I don't know about Woodsy. Why?'

'Just for the record,' Morrissey said. 'Nothing to worry about.' But as he went back upstairs he was reflecting that today was Thursday, and wondering if another boy had taken Duffin's place.

This time, Osgodby was on the point of going out. He said, 'Can it wait, John? I'm a bit pushed,' and when the chief inspector shook his head he sighed and leaned back on the edge of his desk. 'Tell me the worst,' he invited. 'It's one of those days.'

WHEN BARRETT CAME BACK, Morrissey had already set up a watch on the wine bar, and was feeling quietly optimistic.

Barrett swallowed some of his pride and said with defensive meekness, 'Any chance of being briefed on what's happening?'

'Later, Neil; all in good time. Why not go down to the canteen and fill up the inner man? Which WPC did you take by the way?'

'Janet Yarby.'

'Thought you might. Nice lady.' There was a complacent note in the chief inspector's voice that irked Barrett even more. 'Don't forget you still owe her a Mars bar. Off you go then.' He beamed beneficently and, like a raw cadet, the sergeant went.

Morrissey thought about Wellen, and told himself he wasn't going to risk falling into the same mistake that had been made about Goddard, even though the temptation was there. There was nothing to link Wellen with events at Little Henge except a matchbook cover, and that wasn't enough. He was also an odd enough figure to have been noticed even in such an unseeing community as Little Henge.

Restlessly he went back to the file, sure that some of the answers must be there. *Why* had no one been seen at the Hartley cottage when her neighbours seemed to do little else but look out of their windows?

Helen had gone into the village near the time Marion Walsh died; she of all people would have noticed a stranger. He turned back to his own report. Some men had been drinking outside the Bull; also two young mothers and Old Willy had passed by. And the postman had been around. But the postman had been drinking tea with Martha in the little shop.

Two young mothers and Old Willy, walking right past the Walsh house and seeing nothing. No, that was wrong: Willy had been walking up Vicarage Lane. Morrissey went to see if the computer could retrieve the right house-to-house reports from so little, and found it could.

Barrett was back at his desk. 'Sir?'

'Neil?'

Morrissey added more papers to the file, and sat back in his chair. The two unobservant young women had noticed no one, not even Old Willy, and apart from his pub cronies, Old Willy had seen only the vicar. Great! He closed the file and pushed it away from him, and frowned at Barrett.

'It was a good thing you found that woggle, it saved us making a big mistake,' he said. 'I've asked for a second post-mortem on Goddard,' and then he brought the detective sergeant up to date and watched him squirm.

'It seemed . . .'

'Open and shut—I know, Neil. But they're the ones it pays to be careful with. Luckily there aren't many of 'em.'

Barrett said grudgingly, 'If you're right and Goddard wasn't a suicide, it puts us back where we started.'

'Not quite. We've got a probable three more murders,' Morrissey said acidly, and wondered if there were any more.

AT A FEW MINUTES after five a boy went into *Cobblers* by the back door, and Morrissey was satisfied that his decision to wait hadn't been ill-judged. And then he waited another fifteen minutes to give Wellen time to get his cameras set up.

Barrett felt some of the chief inspector's expectancy transfer itself to him. He had become part of the process again, and it was a good feeling to see a purpose in what he was doing. He was even prepared to be forgiving.

At a quarter past five, two detective constables in sweatshirts and jeans went into the wine bar and stood niggling about what to drink. Three from the uniform branch, co-opted into plain clothes, loitered near the back door.

A few minutes later Morrissey and Barrett went in openly, and ignored the barman's frantic plea for them not to go through the bead curtain.

Morrissey made no effort to be silent as he went upstairs. In a big room that ran the length of the building, Wellen had moved out from behind his cameras and looked sick.

'There's nothing illegal,' he said quickly. 'Nothing at all.'

'I'm sure we'll find something,' Morrissey said disgustedly. He looked at the boy. 'Go and get dressed.'

As he scuttled behind a canework screen, the boy had begun to shiver and Barrett saw his skin break out in goose-flesh. He hazarded a guess that it was fright rather than cold that caused the reaction.

Where the boy had stood, a backdrop on the wall showed palm trees and an impossibly azure sea. There was a pile of sand on the floor and a plastic sand-castle self-consciously beside it. The giant beach ball he had been holding bore the legend *Beach Boys*.

Wellen blustered, 'You can't do this: this is private property. Where's your warrant; you haven't got a warrant; if you had you'd have shown it by now.'

'An oversight,' Morrissey said coldly and handed him the folded paper, signed in precise copperplate by a magistrate. The bluster evaporated and Wellen reached for the telephone. Barrett took the instrument away from him.

'You can make a phone call,' he said, '*one* phone call, when we get to the station. Until then you'll just have to be patient.'

'Are you still paying two pounds a session?' Morrissey asked. 'That's what you paid Philip Duffin, isn't it? But I'm curious about the twenty pounds he was going to get for "special" photographs. What were they, Mr Wellen, what made them special?'

'I don't know what you're on about, really I don't. I take art shots, nothing else. You know very well I collect them—they're nice to look at. We've all got our weak spots, haven't we?'

'I'm glad you think that,' said Morrissey, 'because I don't think it will take us too long to find yours, not when we really turn this place upside down.'

Wellen's eyes swivelled round the room where a search had already started. 'Don't break anything,' he said weakly. 'It's expensive stuff.'

Morrissey smiled. 'Worth more than a boy, would you say? What happened to the Duffin boy after you'd taken those "special photographs", Wellen, because he hasn't been seen since?' He turned to Barrett. 'Get him down to the station.'

'Move!' said Barrett, and gave Wellen a small push.

'You'll ruin my business,' Wellen shrieked. 'What will the customers think when they see policemen all over the place?'

Morrissey said acerbically, 'What customers? What business?'

Barrett added, 'They'll think you've been up to something, and they'll be right, won't they? It's called enticement, and you're going to lose your licence at the very least.'

The boy came out from beyond the screen. He looked pale, his grey school uniform was at odds with the room.

Barrett took out his personal radio, and said softly, 'Have the WPC come up now, will you?'

Wellen began to sweat; it started out of the pores of his face, and he wiped his hands down the front of his satin waistcoat. 'You wanted to come, didn't you, Kevin love?' he said feverishly. 'I didn't persuade you, did I?' The boy just looked at him.

Morrissey nodded at Barrett and the sergeant took Wellen's arm and began to move towards the door.

'You haven't told me what you're looking for,' the sweating man protested. 'I've got a right to be told that.'

'It isn't what we're looking for that worries you, is it? It's what you're afraid we might find,' Morrissey said. He saw that the boy was shivering again, and added with sudden savagery, 'That's the trouble with your line of work. When you shovel shit it sticks to your boots and you, Mr Wellen, stink of it.'

TWENTY-NINE

'I'M ALLOWED a phone call,' Wellen said in desperation.

'And you had it,' Barrett told him. 'Not your fault he wasn't in. But just to set your mind at rest you can try again—later.'

'In the meantime,' said Morrissey, 'tell me about these photographs. This one for example, and this, and this and this.' He laid them on the table in front of Wellen as if they were playing cards. 'Of course, these are just a sample, but you know that, you took them. Four boys, Mr Wellen. Four boys we are urgently looking for.'

'Well how am I supposed to know that? What have they done? I didn't know they were in trouble with the law: they seemed nice boys.'

'As I'm sure they were until they met you, Mr Wellen, but then, I wouldn't say you were a force for good where young boys are concerned. Would you?'

'I never forced any of them to come to my place,' Wellen said petulantly, 'and I didn't ask them neither, and you can't charge me with enticement. I want to leave.'

'I'm quite sure you do, but we want you to stay. You're helping us with our enquiries, and if you have a clear conscience you can't object to that, can you?'

'Yes, I can. I've got a good business and your lot are ruining it. If you've damaged any of my equipment . . .'

'You can sue us, Mr Wellen, like any other honest citizen.' Barrett smiled at him. 'Of course, the last time you did that you weren't very successful, but who knows—this time may be different.'

'Last time . . . ?'

'We know a lot about you, Mr Wellen.'

'I've never been convicted. Never.'

'Sad, isn't it?' Barrett said. 'Perhaps we can make this a first, break the mould.'

Sweat glistened in Wellen's stubby hair. 'I'm not saying anything else until I've got a solicitor.'

'That could be a long time, Mr Wellen, and in the meantime my men are still searching,' Morrissey pointed out. 'I'm sure they'll find a lot more for us to talk about. If you helped us with these we might not get as upset about other things.' The interview room felt hot; another half hour and it would be like a sweat box; the heating made things too hot on warm days, too cold in winter.

'What other things?'

Morrissey slid a flat account book onto the table between them. 'My guess would be a bit of brown envelope retailing; and stronger stuff than these,' he touched one of the photographs.

Barrett said, 'It'll be interesting to check his mailing list. Upset a few people.'

'I don't know what you're on about. I told you, I only deal in art shots.'

'But you have "special" customers who like something extra,' Morrissey said. 'And punters who pay to have you procure for them?' He leaned forward across the table and Wellen moved back on his chair. 'This boy, for example. You remember, Mr Wellen?' He rested a finger on Philip Duffin's photograph. 'He came to your studio to have some of those "special" photographs taken by a man he hadn't met before. And that man was going to pay him twenty pounds.' Wellen blinked and stayed silent. 'He hasn't been seen since; why do you think that might be?'

'You haven't charged me, and I haven't been arrested,' Wellen said, 'and I'm not going to talk to you any more.'

There was a knock and Smythe stuck his head in. 'A word?' he said. Morrissey went out.

'What's all that about?' Wellen said. Barrett simply smiled.

Morrissey came back in and told Barrett, 'Arrest him and tell him what his rights are. The charges are possession of obscene material for the purposes of distribution and profit, and procurement and enticement of under-age males. That, as they say, is for starters.'

'I want to ring my solicitor again,' Wellen said as Morrissey went out.

SMYTHE DROVE Morrissey back to the Middlebrook Road. The three police cars parked outside *Cobblers* had drawn knots of onlookers. Nothing changed, Morrissey thought as he went inside; there'd still be a crowd at Tyburn.

Upstairs, in a room behind the backdrop, were piles of magazines, some packeted ready for mailing. Morrissey opened one at random and saw the children. Wellen couldn't say these were art shots, he thought as he stared at a centrefold. The boyish roundness of forehead and cheeks, the almost prettily waving hair contrasted sharply with eyes that were too round; terror did that, this boy wasn't acting.

He felt an aching, searing sadness; the boy could be anybody's son: his! When that thought came he wanted to explode in anger, but all he could do was clamp his jaw tight and hope he was on the edge of the answers he needed.

There were photographs too: some he guessed had been taken by Wellen; others, he could see from the backgrounds, had come from the continent. He turned away.

'Anything else?'

'Another customer list.'

Morrissey sighed and felt a measure of relief. 'I'll take it with me.'

The detective constable passed it to him. 'This was with it,' he said. 'Seems innocent enough, I don't know what to make of it. One of his friends maybe?' He showed Morrissey the photograph of a man crossing the road in front of *Cobblers*. 'Don't seem the sort of thing he'd keep in a safe.'

The chief inspector looked at it; a black and white photograph taken from above, slightly blurred. A tall man in a dark sweatsuit, with sunglasses and peaked cap hiding part of his face. But it didn't hide enough, thought Morrissey, and he saw everything smoothly drop into place.

THIRTY

WELLEN HAD BEEN taken down to the cells; Morrissey had him brought back to the interview room.

'I think in your own best interests it's time you decided to talk to us,' the chief inspector said, and laid the second address book on the table. 'Of course that isn't all we found.' He stared at the round face and wanted to see it fill with terror, like the child's in the magazine had. He put the file copy of Ian Pallister's photograph, proud in his scout uniform, in front of Wellen. 'This boy is missing too. I don't think we shall find him alive.'

Wellen's eyes panicked. 'I didn't take that,' he said.

'No,' Morrissey agreed. 'Not your work. But that isn't to say you never knew him, is it? Five missing boys, Mr Wellen. Where would you be looking if you were me?'

'You've got it all wrong,' Wellen rubbed his hands on his knees. 'I didn't touch any of them. There's a difference between touching and looking. I take photographs, I sell photographs. Nothing else.'

Morrissey looked at Barrett.

The sergeant said, 'Not true. You enticed boys, these boys,' he put the other four photographs on the table, 'to pose obscenely.'

'And not just for yourself, Mr Wellen,' Morrissey added. 'You rented them to punters and if I don't get their names you could find yourself facing very serious charges indeed.'

Barrett said, 'You'll be too old to press the shutter when you come out. Think about that.'

'I've never seen this one,' Wellen pushed Pallister's photograph back across the table. 'And how am I supposed to know the others are missing? No one ever told me.'

'We've told you now,' said Barrett. 'What are you going to do about it?'

Morrissey suggested. 'Let me tell you what it looks like from our side. You knew Marion Walsh a long time ago, and we know Mrs Walsh came to see you at *Cobblers* because we found one of your match-books at her home. Now this lady died very violently, Mr Wellen, and so did her daily help. If you add to that the fact that she sometimes employed a little blackmail to increase her income, where do you suppose it leads us?'

'It leads us to think she was blackmailing you,' Barrett said.

Morrissey smiled wolfishly. 'It leads us to you and five missing boys.'

Wellen's head shook agitatedly. 'No,' he whimpered, 'I didn't even recognise her until she said who she was. She wanted to know about...' He stopped. Morrissey watched a drip of sweat trickle from Wellen's hairline to the socket of his eye.

'About this man?' The chief inspector showed him the photograph of the man crossing Middlebrook Road. 'She'd seen him come into the bar, hadn't she, and she wanted to know why?'

Wellen crumbled.

'His name,' Morrissey said. 'Let's save time.'

'Oh God, I wish I hadn't kept it. He said his name was Barlow and it was only the one boy.'

'This boy?' Morrissey's finger moved to Duffin's photograph.

'Yes.'

'And the boy knew him?'

'No. Well . . . he might have done.' Wellen shifted. 'He looked a bit surprised when I went in with Barlow, and I thought he was going to say something.'

'And then?'

'Wasn't my business. I went out.'

'They left together?'

'I didn't see.'

'You don't see much at all, do you?' Morrissey snapped impatiently. 'I'm wasting my time.'

'I know where the other three are,' Wellen said sickly. 'They're down in London.' Morrissey remembered Jason's boast and said wearily, 'The magazines. Get the addresses down, Neil, and let the Met know.'

'For God's sake, don't say it came from me,' Wellen pleaded. 'I'll be dead.' Morrissey only looked, but Wellen didn't speak again.

BARRETT HAD HELD the photograph in his hand before they had talked to Wellen the second time, and hadn't wanted to believe Morrissey. But the chief had put out an urgent request for information, and it had come in while they were in the interview room. He thought about Goddard and felt sick.

'You weren't to know, Neil,' Morrissey said. 'Everything pointed to you being right.'

'But I wasn't,' said Barrett. 'Two previous offences and three months' psychiatric treatment; why didn't we know?'

'Because no one wanted us to. Next time they'll think twice,' the chief inspector said.

'I still don't see why he killed Betty Hartley.'

'With a nose for gossip like she had, once he'd decided Marion had to go he'd no real option. He couldn't take the risk she knew what had been going on.'

Osgodby had just got back from his meeting.

'It might save time if you just moved up here permanently, John,' he said dryly when Morrissey went in. 'Want some coffee?' He got another mug and tipped the jug. 'Bit strong.'

Morrissey laid out the facts, and Osgodby said, 'You'd better be damned sure, John. This will have to go through the chief constable, and it's going to cause a lot of trouble for a lot of people.'

'It already has,' said Morrissey, 'and I'm sure. The damage can't be helped. It might encourage less laxity in future.' He told himself there was too much turning of the other cheek, too many second chances. He looked at Osgodby. 'If it hadn't been for the cleverness of Goddard's faked suicide we would've got round to him. The answer was there if we'd had time to look.'

'And the boys,' said Osgodby. 'Do you know where to look for them?' Morrissey nodded painfully.

'I'll need two exhumation orders, but I don't know which graves yet,' he said. 'We'll find out from the Registrar.'

Osgodby shuffled. 'You're owed an apology about Goddard,' he said abruptly. 'You have it.'

Morrissey nodded and went out.

BARTHOLOMEW SEEMED surprised when he opened the door to them and found two uniformed policemen standing behind Morrissey and Barrett.

'Come in, Chief Inspector,' he said politely, 'though I'm not sure what I can do for you.'

Morrissey and Barrett stepped into the wide, cold hallway, and Barrett moved past the vicar. As Bartholomew glanced from one to the other, awareness came into his eyes. He didn't try to move away. 'You know,' he said flatly. Then he said, 'Who has most importance: a man of God or a gossip and a whore? They would have destroyed me, chief inspector, and God wouldn't permit that. He told me what to do and I carried out His commands.'

'And the Duffin boy,' Morrissey said, 'whose only sin was to recognise you. How did God feel about that?'

'He is my right hand and I am His.' Impassively Bartholomew heard Morrissey charge and caution him. 'I won't be harmed,' he said, 'you'll see that, Chief Inspector. God will always protect his Priest.'

Barrett watched him walk away between the two uniformed men. 'Insane?' he said doubtfully. A billow of wind caught the black cassock and filled it like a sail.

Morrissey thought of the darkness beyond the door in Marjorie Cotton's paintings. Had Bartholomew come downstairs, not knowing she was there and left the flapping cassock in her mind? And had it snapped then, or when she saw Marion on the floor, or when she grasped the broken bottle and cut the face of her husband's mistress to shreds?

Bartholomew's crushing blow would have brought death within minutes, but to be soaked in blood as she had been, Mrs Cotton must have wielded the broken bottle herself.

He answered Barrett's question. 'That's what he'll try for; it's worked before. Let's hope he doesn't make it.' There was a raw anger inside him as he thought about the crime he saw as more than a crime. Child murder lent a new level of insanity to a world already half mad. In his head, the chief inspector could be judge, jury, and executioner; coldly, at that moment. Maybe later he would doubt that, but not now. He wished he could see a sense and purpose in all things, but here at the end of an investigation he saw only chaos.

On the white-painted wall a crucifix hung, and a ray of sun falling through the coloured leaded lights of the hall window set a multi-hued pattern around it. Morrissey remembered the butterflies in Bartholomew's study. For a second both images merged, and then deliberately he turned his eyes away.

He wondered what priestly conscience could forgive such sins as Bartholomew's, and send him to an unwarned parish to sin some more.

Through the still open door he watched Bartholomew driven away towards Malminster.

Barrett asked, 'What did we miss?'

'Not miss,' the chief inspector answered. 'Just misinterpreted. Helen Goddard saw the vicar cross Hill Road that first morning. It was *assumed* he'd come from the vicarage, but it was probably the Walsh house. The cassock and the collar got in the way; I believed him when he said Betty Hartley had been expecting a friend, and neither of us picked up on Old Willy.'

Barrett said, 'Old Willy?' Light dawned and he threw up his fists. 'Oh sod it! Bartholomew should have been in Stenton when Marion died.'

'And Old Willy told us he walked up Vicarage Lane and saw him,' finished Morrissey. 'See how easy it is to be wise after the event.'

A little later they found the attic room where Bartholomew had acted out his fantasies, its walls covered with posters and blown-up photographs. In neatly ordered drawers were still pictures and slides, and stacked reels of film lay on a shelf.

Barrett felt his bile rise at the warped sadism on display. He glanced at Morrissey and guessed at the explosion of anger being held down. The sergeant bit his tongue and kept silent. Later, he saw the still pictures of Philip Duffin and Ian Pallister taken after death—and there were others too, some, from their haircuts, reaching back to the seventies—and felt that he had suddenly grown old.

MORRISSEY HAD come away from the initial hearing satisfied that Bartholomew had been remanded for trial by Crown Court. His solicitor had already made the suggestion that he was unfit to plead. All Morrissey could hope was that it was thrown out.

The bodies of both boys had been found under the coffins of two recent burials; one in Stenton churchyard, the other at Little Henge.

Unless Bartholomew told them, it would be impossible to know for certain how the scarf ring had come into Marion Walsh's hands, but she had undoubtedly used it to blackmail him. Why had she condoned such a thing? Morrissey had given up trying to understand. Had she guessed she was blackmailing a psychopath?

Helen Goddard stopped him outside the court room. 'I'm selling the house,' she said. 'I want to get away from Little Henge.' She was standing two steps higher than he and was almost on a level with him. Without warning she leaned forward and kissed him full on the mouth. 'I could love you very easily, Chief Inspector,' she said and hurried past him. And he could very easily let her, he realised, feeling himself stir. The thought that he wouldn't see her again laid bare a small patch of desolation in his mind.

He took Margaret a dozen roses, and because they were out of season had to pay an exorbitant price; but she was pleased, and he enjoyed her pleasure. Since Bartholomew had been arrested she had struggled with the same burden Morrissey had carried for most of his adult life; but for her it was new and frightening. And there would be many more people in the three parishes Bartholomew had served facing the same questions.

MIKE AND KATIE came home together; Katie sniffed at the roses, said, 'Nice,' and looked suspiciously at her parents.

Morrissey grinned.

'Mike,' he said, knowing it would annoy Katie to be ignored, 'I've got two tickets for Wembley on Saturday. American football.'

'Redskins and Eagles!' It was a whoop of joy. 'That's great. How'd you get them?' Morrissey tapped the side of his nose. It hadn't been difficult but it would please Mike to think that it had.

'Great,' said Katie. 'Roses for Mum, tickets for Mike. Get lost, Katie; you're a jerk.' She flounced to the door and Morrissey let her go. A few minutes later he heard her squeal, and then the monotonous beat of the new Julian Cope album he had left on her bed came through the ceiling.

'She found it,' said Margaret.

'She found it,' he agreed with a grimace, and allowed his conscience to slide quietly back to sleep.

D · A · T · E

WITH A DEAD

D O C T O R

T O N I · B R I L L

Midge Cohen's mother has fixed her up again. What would it hurt to meet this nice Jewish doctor, a urologist even, and give him a try, she insists.

But all Dr. Leon Skripnik wants from Midge, an erstwhile Russian scholar, is a translation of a letter he's received from the old country. To get rid of him she agrees to his request. The next morning, he's found dead.

"An engaging first novel. A warm, observant, breezy talent is evident here."

—*Kirkus Reviews*

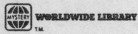

ERIC WRIGHT

"Clap hands, here comes Charlie...in Eric Wright's excellent series."
—*New York Times Book Review*

IT'LL MAKE A KILLING AT THE BOX OFFICE...

Acts of sabotage are throwing a major film off financial kilter. Inspector Charlie Salter finds his glamorous job as watchdog turning sinister as fake fire alarms, muggings, damaged equipment, stolen film and the kidnapping of an actor heat up production.

When the film's writer is found stabbed to death in a compromising position, Salter delves into underlying layers of greed, ambition and burning revenge as he races to find a killer who will stop at nothing to kill the film... or anybody who gets in the way.

"Charlie Salter is a likeable and savvy police veteran."
—*Publishers Weekly*

NOT AVAILABLE IN CANADA

FINAL

 MYSTERY **WORLDWIDE LIBRARY**®

FINAL CUT

Take 2 books and a surprise gift FREE

SPECIAL LIMITED-TIME OFFER

Mail to: The Mystery Library™
               3010 Walden Ave.
               P.O. Box 1867
               Buffalo, N.Y. 14269-1867

YES! Please send me 2 free books from the Mystery Library™ and my free surprise gift. Then send me 2 mystery books, first time in paperback, every month. Bill me only $3.74 per book plus 25¢ delivery and applicable sales tax, if any*. There is no minimum number of books I must purchase. I can always return a shipment at your cost simply by dropping it in the mail, or cancel at any time. Even if I never buy another book from The Mystery Library™, the 2 free books and surprise gift are mine to keep forever.
                                                              414 BPY AFND

Name   (PLEASE PRINT)

Address   Apt. No.

City   State   Zip

OTHER PEOPLE'S HOUSES

SUSAN ROGERS COOPER

In Prophesy County, Oklahoma, the unlikely event of a homicide is coupled with the likely event that if one occurs, the victim is somebody everybody knows....

And everybody knows nice bank teller Lois Bell who, along with her husband and three kids, dies of accidental carbon monoxide poisoning. But things just aren't sitting right with chief deputy Milton Kovak. Why were the victims' backgrounds completely untraceable? And why was the federal government butting its nose in the case?

"Milt Kovak tells his story with a voice that's as comforting as a rocking chair and as salty as a fisherman."

—*Houston Chronicle*

First Time In Paperback

MIRIAM BORGENICHT

A tragedy turns into a living nightmare when health counselor Linda Stewart's adopted infant daughter is legally reclaimed by the baby's natural teenage mother—and both are found dead two days later.

Linda's agonizing grief is channeled into a burning determination to solve these senseless murders. While suspicions of drug involvement might explain the sudden fortune the young mother had acquired, Linda's subtle probing takes a seedy turn into black-market adoptions.

"Borgenicht's perceptive comments on troubling social issues generate plenty of tension." —Publishers Weekly